Secrets Revealed

By

USA Today Bestselling Author

ROBERTA KAGAN

Book Two in The Eidel's Story Series

Copyright © 2016 by Roberta Kagan

All rights reserved. No part of this publication may be reproduced, distributed, or transmitted in any form or by any means, including photocopying, recording, or other electronic or mechanical methods, without the prior written permission of the publisher, except in the case of brief quotations embodied in critical reviews and certain other noncommercial uses permitted by copyright law.

CONTACT ME

I love hearing from readers, so feel free to drop me an email telling me your thoughts about the book or series.

Email: roberta@robertakagan.com

Please sign up for my mailing list, and you will receive Free short stories including an USA Today award-winning novella as my gift to you!!!!! To sign up…

Check out my website http://www.robertakagan.com.

Come and like my Facebook page!

https://www.facebook.com/roberta.kagan.9

Join my book club

https://www.facebook.com/groups/1494285400798292/?ref=br_rs

Follow me on BookBub to receive automatic emails whenever I am offering a special price, a freebie, a giveaway, or a new release. Just click the link below, then click follow button to the right of my name. Thank you so much for your interest in my work.

https://www.bookbub.com/authors/roberta-kagan.

DISCLAIMER

This is a work of fiction. Names, characters, businesses, places, events, and incidents are either the products of the author's imagination or used in a fictitious manner. Any resemblance to actual persons, living or dead, or actual events are purely coincidental.

TABLE OF CONTENTS

CONTACT ME..3
DISCLAIMER 4
TABLE OF CONTENTS...5
PROLOGUE...8
CHAPTER ONE 10
CHAPTER TWO 23
CHAPTER THREE 25
CHAPTER FOUR..30
CHAPTER FIVE 34
CHAPTER SIX..44
CHAPTER SEVEN..48
CHAPTER EIGHT 65
CHAPTER NINE 72
CHAPTER TEN..84
CHAPTER ELEVEN..88
CHAPTER TWELVE 96
CHAPTER THIRTEEN 98
CHAPTER FOURTEEN 100
CHAPTER FIFTEEN 106
CHAPTER SIXTEEN 108
CHAPTER SEVENTEEN 112
CHAPTER EIGHTEEN 114
CHAPTER NINETEEN...115

CHAPTER TWENTY	123
CHAPTER TWENTY-ONE	124
CHAPTER TWENTY-TWO	136
CHAPTER TWENTY-THREE	137
CHAPTER TWENTY-FOUR	144
CHAPTER TWENTY-FIVE	153
CHAPTER TWENTY-SIX	155
CHAPTER TWENTY-SEVEN	160
CHAPTER TWENTY-EIGHT	165
CHAPTER TWENTY-NINE	171
CHAPTER THIRTY	176
CHAPTER THIRTY-ONE	179
CHAPTER THIRTY-TWO	185
CHAPTER THIRTY-THREE	187
CHAPTER THIRTY-FOUR	198
CHAPTER THIRTY-FIVE	201
CHAPTER THIRTY-SIX	204
CHAPTER THIRTY-SEVEN	205
CHAPTER THIRTY-EIGHT	211
CHAPTER THIRTY-NINE	219
CHAPTER FOURTY	236
CHAPTER FOURTY-ONE	261
CHAPTER FOURTY-TWO	266
Authors Note	270
MORE BOOKS BY THE AUTHOR AVAILABLE ON AMAZON	272

PROLOGUE

Warsaw, Poland, 1946

Poland suffered greatly when it was taken over by Hitler. The Polish people found themselves living in terror under the thumb of the Third Reich. Many of the citizens of Poland refused to accept the Nazi rule and so they formed a resistance group called the Home Army. In October of 1944, there was an uprising of the Home Army against the Nazis in Warsaw. Joseph Stalin promised to send Russian troops to assist the Polish in their rebellion. He kept that promise, and a war in the streets ensued between the Nazis and the Polish, with the assistance of Russia. The Home Army put up a valiant effort but, in the end, suffered great losses and were defeated.

Meanwhile, Hitler's army was taking a brutal beating from the Allies. In addition, Hitler never calculated for the weather or the vast terrain his soldiers would face during a winter on the Eastern front. By 1945, the Nazis surrendered. The Americans and British marched through the previously Nazi-occupied territory from the west, while the Soviets came coursing through from the east. Although Stalin had proclaimed friendship to Poland during its Nazi occupation, Russia now became Poland's conqueror. And so the Nazi flags with the black swastikas that had been hung throughout Poland, striking fear in the hearts of the Polish people, were torn down. But in their place there rose another flag, not the Polish flag, but one that bore the image of a hammer and a sickle. Poland still was not free; she now belonged to Russia. When Stalin spoke he promised a better life under communist rule. However, his words were meaningless, evaporating as if they were never spoken, like drops of moisture on leaves the morning after a rainstorm. The blatant truth was that, although Hitler and his terrible Third Reich were gone, the Polish were not free. They were now under communist occupation.

CHAPTER ONE

1956 Warsaw, Poland, ten years later.

Helen walked into her small but tidy apartment. In her hand she carried a cloth bag. Inside were a few potatoes and carrots, two meat bones to make a soup, and a loaf of bread. She set the bag down on the table. Lately, she had taken to going to the bakery and buying bread rather than baking it. Since she and the baker's wife had become friendly, Helen was getting a nice discount on day-old bread. This almost made buying it more cost-effective than baking, and it certainly was easier. Helen slipped off her coat and hung it on a hook by the door and began unloading her bag. Ela would be home from her classes in an hour and, as always, Helen liked to clean the vegetables and have the soup in a kettle simmering when Ela arrived. If everything was done, Helen would have some time before dinner to sew with her daughter or just enjoy a cup of tea and talk about the events of their day.

Peel a carrot, chop a potato; Helen glanced out the window. The neighborhood children, just home from school, were gathering in the courtyard. Helen remembered when Ela was just a child. She missed those days terribly. Ela was going to be seventeen. How the time flies; she is already a woman.

There was a soft, almost timid knock at the door. Helen thought nothing of it. The neighbors who lived in the building came to visit her quite often. Sometimes they needed to borrow an onion, other times they were just lonely and in need of a few minutes of human companionship. She dried her hands on a dishtowel and opened the door. Her smile dropped as her hand went to her throat. In her doorway stood a man, an old friend, someone from a life she'd lived long ago. A man whom she hadn't seen in over ten years. Time and war had weathered him, but he was alive.

"Artur? Artur Labecki?" Helen said, her

voice cracking. "How are you? Come in, come in…" She opened the door wide and motioned him in with her hand.

He entered. His coat sleeves were frayed, and the skin on his face had gone floppy, falling into deep lines that made him look older than his forty-five years.

"I am all right." Artur smiled. "I am glad to see you, Helen. You look well."

"Sit down, please. Can I get you a cup of tea or coffee?"

"No, no thank you. I have wanted to come and see you for some time. But, I couldn't. Maci would never have accepted me coming here to see you."

"How is Maci?"

"She passed away this last winter."

"I'm sorry."

"Yes, I was too. She was a good woman. Not always a good wife to me. But, certainly a strong woman. Perhaps she was too strong for me. I've often wondered about that. Did you know that she fought right alongside the men in the home army during the Warsaw uprising?"

"I didn't know. But I do remember how beautiful she was."

"She was, wasn't she? She was a terrible flirt. That's probably why she didn't want me coming to see you. Maci always had problems staying faithful and so she always assumed I did too. Maci constantly accused me of having a little crush on you."

Helen gave a nervous laugh.

"I suppose maybe I did have at least a little attraction to you. Why not? You're a beautiful woman. But, at the time, you were married to Nik and he was my best friend. I would never have done that to him."

"Yes, poor Nik. I do miss him." She whispered, "I don't know how it happened, but things went so wrong between Nik and me."

"Yes, I know. He told me often that you two were having problems. And besides, I had a good idea that things were awry when Eryk was arrested and you came to me wanting to see him. Still, Nik was a good friend. We all lost so many of our friends during the Nazi takeover, didn't we?"

"Oh yes. The Nazis. They took so much from all of us. It was a merciless time. Did you know that I lost my son Lars, too? The food was so scarce that when Lars and Nik got sick, they were both so thin that their bodies didn't have the strength to fight the disease.

"Terribly sad what happened to everyone we knew. You know Nik never trusted the Russians. He always said he didn't like Stalin's face," Artur said, then he shrugged his shoulders. "I was a fool. I trusted Stalin when he promised to help the Home Army."

"You weren't alone. Plenty of people believed Russia would help free us from the Germans."

"Yes, well, Stalin has been dead for three years and Russia still holds our beloved Poland in her grip." Artur shook his head. He continued, "But, quite frankly, I didn't come here to talk to you about Nik. That is not why I have come to see you, Helen. I'm here because of Eryk."

"Eryk?"

Her voice trembled. Just the mention of his name, even though he'd been dead for many years, still made her heart flutter. Helen knew that Eryk was undoubtedly the one true love of her life.

"Before the Nazis hung Eryk he put this necklace in my hand and made me promise I would somehow make sure that it got to you. He said to tell you that you must give it to Ela when she was old enough to understand." Artur took a small gold star of David that hung on a chain out of the breast pocket of his coat. "I don't know anymore. That was all he said. He never explained why you would want this for Ela. In fact, I have no idea where he got it from. However, I made a vow to him that I would bring it to you if I survived the war. So, here." Artur handed Helen the necklace. Helen felt an icy finger tickle her spine as the chain touched her fingers. The bright gold metal felt cold in her hand. She wasn't completely certain where Eryk had gotten this piece of jewelry but she had to believe that it had belonged to Zofia. Eryk was the only living person other than herself that knew the truth about Ela. Not even Ela knew. But Helen had shared her deepest secrets with Eryk. And one night she told him the truth … that she was not Ela's mother. In fact, Ela's birth mother was a Jew in the Warsaw ghetto and her name was Zofia Weiss.

Perhaps somehow in Eryk's work with the underground, he'd met Zofia and she'd given him the necklace. Helen knew that Eryk was working with the underground helping Jews to escape.

But now how am I ever going to explain all of this to Ela? She has grown up believing that I am her mother. What will she think if she learns the truth? How will she feel about me? About Zofia? About herself? She's so involved in the Catholic church. That's my fault. I raised her to be my child, not Zofia's. Have I done her a disservice? Dear God, I would never want to hurt Ela. I could hide this necklace away in a drawer and never say another word about It ... I could ... couldn't I?

"Thank you. Eryk said nothing about how he got this or why he wanted me to give it to Ela?"

"No, I am sorry, Helen. I don't have any more information for you. There wasn't time for him to talk to me about it. He slipped it into my hand on the morning of his execution. You see, I bribed a guard to let me say goodbye to him. Eryk and I had less than a minute together before they took him out to hang him. Then, as you know, he died in the square."

"I remember."

"You were there. Right in front. I saw you there."

"Yes, I was there. I went because I thought he needed me. I wanted him to see me, to look into my eyes one last time. I hoped it would give him some comfort."

"The two of you were lovers, weren't you?" Artur asked.

Helen nodded. She cast her eyes to the ground, ashamed of having had an affair while she was married and of breaking one of God's commandments. But, there was no point in keeping it a secret anymore. Eryk and Nik were both dead. And she hated herself for it, but she'd sinned far worse than having a love affair with Eryk.

"I thought so," Artur whispered. "A lot of things happened during that time period that we probably would never have done otherwise. But it's all in the past now."

"Yes, it is," Helen said, and she thought of Rolf the Nazi bastard who had taken her body and soul. The time she'd spent with him was the worst sin of all. She hated him and knew that she should have refused him. But she dared not. He had known about Ela and he could easily have taken the little girl and sent her to a concentration camp or worse. So she'd let him do as he pleased with her. That was what drove Eryk to kill him. And then Eryk had paid for the crime with his life.

"I won't ask you to try to explain anything. I

don't need to know. But we are old friends, Helen. I am a lonely man now that Maci has passed on. She was my best friend. I know everyone thought she was a little bit loose, but I understood her. It was just her nature to be that way with men. She was unfaithful, but I forgave her. I loved her, Helen. I am lost now. And, I know this may sound very bold and even coarse, if it does I am sorry. But I was thinking that maybe, if you are not too busy, we could have dinner one night …"

She studied him. He was wringing his hands. Poor Artur. It seemed she'd known him forever. They had all been such good friends before the war, she and Nik, Artur and Maci. Helen had always secretly envied Maci, who was a beautiful, glamorous girl. Even so, until the Labeckis invited the Dobinskis to a meeting of the Home Army, the couples had been great friends. But then once Artur had made it clear that he was a part of the resistance, Nik began to distance himself from the Labeckis. Nik wanted no part of the Home Army. And so, for a while, the Dobinskis and the Labeckis didn't spend much time together. But Helen remembered Artur's involvement with the resistance. So when the Nazis were about to hang Eryk, in desperation, not knowing where else to turn, Helen went to see Artur. She was hoping he would be able to find a way for her to see Eryk one last time. He had been unable to help.

"Dinner?" she said sighing. "I don't know Artur. I am not sure how I feel about all of this. I don't go out with men. I stay at home at night with Ela. I've given up on romance. That sort of thing is for the young."

"You're still young, Helen."

"Maybe in age, but certainly not in my heart or soul. I don't want to feel that way towards anyone again."

"Helen," he said looking her square in the eye. "I can keep a secret. That much you know about me from our past. If you don't want Ela to know about the necklace, you don't have to worry. She will never hear about it from me."

How did he know I was worried about him

telling Ela about the necklace? Or him mentioning Eryk in front of Ela? He knew that I wanted him to walk back out that door and get out of my life because if he said the wrong thing it could open a Pandora's box and then Ela would ask a million uncomfortable questions. Questions that could change her life, our lives. But…Artur is telling the truth when he says that he can keep a secret. Artur never told Nik about me coming to see him concerning Eryk. He could have told him. But he never did. He kept my secret then and if he says he will keep it now I have to believe him. And, oddly enough, it does feel good to see an old familiar face. The memories Artur and I share are long and deep. It would be nice to have someone to talk to, someone who understands my past because he too has lived through the Nazi occupation. Looking into Artur's eyes helps me to feel less alone in the sadness of all of my secrets.

"I am not proposing marriage. Come on Helen, It's just a meal between old friends," he said, his eyes twinkling with hope. "I need a friend, Helen. An old friend…a friend who still remembers what life was like before the Nazis."

She hesitated for a moment. "Dinner? I'm sorry Artur. I can't."

"I won't give up on you, Helen."

"You must. I can't, Artur."

CHAPTER TWO

At seventeen, Ela was a beautiful young woman. Petite and slender with golden curls that she wore pulled away from her face in a ponytail. But unlike most girls her age, Ela cared very little for her physical appearance. She was dedicated to her life's mission. Ela felt in her heart that she had heard a calling. Several nights she'd awakened, sure she had heard the voice of God beckoning to her to come to him, to join the convent. Since she was a young child she'd admired the nuns. They were filled with conviction and true devotion. Ela had always felt confused about what she was meant to do with her life and it was their sureness that had always appealed to her. Sometimes they were harsh towards her, but she didn't mind. They knew things she did not. She was convinced of it and she often wondered how they knew they were meant to become nuns.

Then it happened.

She began to have the dreams. And once she heard the voices, everything she was meant to do with her life became clear to her. Ela had not yet told her mother of her plans to join the convent. But she was sure that Helen would approve of her choice. Helen had taken her to church since she was a small child even though it had been dangerous to do so when the Nazis were in power. It was because of Helen's determination to familiarize her with Catholicism that Ela believed Helen would be overjoyed that Ela had heard the calling. Tonight, when they were eating dinner, Ela planned to surprise her mother with the good news.

CHAPTER THREE

"You want to become a nun?" Helen said. Perhaps this was God's way of letting her know that she had done the right thing by taking her into the church.

He is forgiving my sins. At least I hope that is what this is about. Still there is that unfinished business of lying to Ela about her Jewish heritage.

"Yes, Mother. I hear God speaking to me in my dreams. I am sure now that this is what I was meant to do. I've found a convent where I can begin my postulancy. It is right here in Warsaw."

Helen knew exactly where the convent was and the location brought on a fresh pang of guilt. The convent was located less than a mile from where the Warsaw Ghetto had been erected, where Zofia had been imprisoned and from where, on one dark night, Ela was whisked away from the terrible fate that awaited so many other innocent Jewish children.

The soup in Helen's mouth suddenly became difficult to swallow. Ela looked at her mother with eyes of hope and promise. Of course, Ela was just a child. She could never remember that she had been smuggled out of that very same ghetto. She could never understand the importance of the fact that the blood of the Jewish people ran through her veins. Helen forced a half smile.

Is God pleased? Is that why Ela is hearing voices? Or is God angry that I have kept the truth from her? She has a right to know and yet I cannot bear the changes that will come to both of us once she learns the truth.

"I woke up last night sweating even though it is not particularly hot outside. I thought I heard a voice, but I couldn't tell if it was a dream or if I had actually heard it. Do you know what I mean? The voice was clear, very clear. It said that my heart and soul belong to God. It was a woman's voice who said all of that. And then she told me that she loves me. I closed my eyes and saw a vision of a dark-haired woman. She smiled at me. I thought it must be the Mother Mary."

The Mother Mary? What if it wasn't that at all? What if it was Zofia?

"What did she look like? The woman, I mean?"

"She looked strangely familiar, as if I'd seen her before. Although I cannot remember where or when. Maybe it was in a painting I saw of the Virgin Mother. Anyway, she was very slender with long, dark curly hair."

Zofia.

That's Zofia. I must be going mad with guilt, Helen thought. "Is this what you want? Do you want to be a nun?"

"Yes, I believe that this is what God wants for me. The church has always given you so much comfort, Mother. I can still remember how it gave us both relief when Papa and Lars died. I want to feel that ease for the rest of my days."

"You are aware that if you become a sister

you will never have a husband or children of your own."

"Yes, I know and that part is very confusing to me because I have always wanted children. But... I keep thinking about the voice I heard."

"But the voice didn't tell you to join the convent, did it?"

"No, not exactly. But I thought that because I heard a voice from beyond telling me that God loves me that it means I am meant to spend my life serving the Lord. So, do I have your blessing, Mother?"

"You have my blessing. If this is what you want, then it is what I want as well," she said, but she thought about the star of David necklace that Artur had given her and wondered again how Eryk had gotten it. It had to be from Zofia.

Ela is better off if she never finds out that her mother was Jewish. Life is and has always been harder for Jews. She believes that she has heard the calling of the church but I am afraid she had a dream about Zofia. Perhaps, Zofia, wherever she is, has died.

Who knows?

I can't know everything. Is this what is best for Ela? I don't know. I don't know.

CHAPTER FOUR

Helen had grown up Catholic with a high regard for those who chose to serve the church. Because of that, she felt that she should be very pleased with Ela's choice to join the convent. However, that night, before she got into bed, she took out the Star of David necklace that she was convinced had once belonged to Ela's mother and held it in her hand. The gold felt cool against her palm and yet it burned a hole within her.

I've lied to the person who means the most to me of anyone in the world. I lied because I love her and I don't want to lose her. If she finds out the truth she may devote herself to a search for Zofia. This could only bring her unhappiness. If she finds Zofia then she must declare herself a Jew. It was horrific for Jews under the Nazis. However, it is still not good under the Communists. And life as a Jew is dangerous. At any time, any government can turn on them. I watched as my neighbors turned people in to the Nazis. These were people they'd known all of their lives. It's a treacherous life for a Jewish person. I loved Zofia, so I took Ela and did my best for her. But so many others didn't care. In fact, they turned their faces away when the Jews were being persecuted. Who is to say such a thing won't happen again? And if it does, isn't Ela better off not knowing she is Jewish? Isn't she safer?

Helen sat down on the edge of her bed and looked out the window at the night sky.

Still, she thought. How can I go on deceiving the child whom I love? How can I allow her to go through with her vocation without first telling her the truth? And even though I must tell her, I am terrified. I cannot imagine how she will feel about me knowing that we have spent our lives together in a world built on lies.

The following day, Helen tried to reveal the truth to Ela but she couldn't seem to find the right moment. She was so afraid of losing Ela's trust.

After dinner, Ela was sewing with a needle

and thread and Helen was knitting a gray scarf. Both had a cup of tea in front of them as they sat together in the living room of the apartment in Warsaw where Ela had grown up.

"Ela..."

"Yes, Mother?"

"There is something I must tell you."

Ela put her sewing down and looked up at Helen. The lines in Helen's forehead were deep with worry. "Please tell me, Mother."

"I don't know how to talk about this with you. I am not sure what to say. How can I break this to you ..." Helen seemed to be talking more to herself than to Ela.

"Mama?" Ela had been calling Helen mother since she turned seventeen. But tonight, seeing Helen so unnerved sent Ela reeling back to her childhood. She felt the same familiar fears she'd felt as a little girl when she would hear Helen and Nik, her papa, arguing about the Nazis when they thought she was asleep. She hadn't understood or remembered much of what they said. But the fearful uneasy feeling that came over her when she would overhear them was still present in her life. During those times she'd always sensed that Papa didn't like her, although she never knew why. But as she heard their angry whispers she would softly say to the empty room, "Mama, I love you. No matter what Papa is saying that is hurting you, you will always have me. I will always be here for you whenever you need me."

"Yes, my sweetheart," Helen said, walking over to Ela and touching her golden hair. When Ela was little, Helen had brushed and brushed her hair, winding the curls around her fingers.

"Please … whatever it is, just tell me …"

"It's a very long story…" Helen said.

"I'm listening, Mama. I'm here for you, no matter what you tell me."

CHAPTER FIVE

Kiev, September 1941

Thirteen-year-old Dovid Levi lay in his bed listening through the wall as his parents whispered in the next room. The walls of his home were thin and he had found it easy to eavesdrop on them for as long as he could remember. He'd learned a lot of things a boy his age wasn't supposed to know by doing just that. After his parents thought he was asleep, they began to speak freely.

One night his mother told his father about the Shanda, the shame his aunt Martha had brought on the family when she began to see the man who lived across the street. She was so embarrassed, his mother had declared. Dovid wasn't sure what had happened between his aunt and the neighbor, but he knew it was something that was a juicy secret, and that made it all the more interesting to him. Another time he learned that one of the girls he knew from Shul had become pregnant out of wedlock. His mother said how she pitied the girl's parents. Dovid had seen the girl. She was pretty with dark wavy hair. He wondered who the boy was. He pressed his ear closer to the wall, but neither of his parents revealed the boy's name.

Perhaps they don't know, he thought.

But Dovid did wonder what it would be like to be that boy. How would it feel to hold a girl in his arms and make a baby? Thinking about this made his face feel hot with curiosity and desire.

I should be ashamed of myself, he thought. But still, sometimes when he was at school his mind would drift to a daydream of that pretty dark-haired girl, soft and naked in his arms. Immediately he would feel guilty. Over the years he'd discovered so many things about life just by listening to his parents through his bedroom wall. However, tonight he didn't need to listen to his parents through the wall to know that his father was worried. Dovid and his father were close. After school, Dovid helped his father at his medical practice. They worked well together. Over the last few weeks Dovid could sense that something was weighing heavily on his Papa's mind. Dovid liked to hear people talk about his Papa. Everyone said that Levi was the most respected doctor in the Jewish sector of Kiev.

"He's a real mench."

"What a kind man, a learned man."

"Such a good doctor with a good heart."

These were some of the things Dovid heard said about his Papa and it made his heart swell with pride.

After the communists took over Russia, medical assistance for the poor became a disaster. The good quality hospitals and doctors were reserved for the government officials but the hospitals that were built for the ordinary people, the workers, were a nightmare. There were constant jokes amongst the working class about the medical care system. They said that the workers' hospitals were places to go if one wanted to die, not if one wanted to be cured. It was quite simple. If a patient in a "people's" hospital did not have the money to bribe the nurses they would not get any care. Instead, they would be left to either heal on their own or die. Menachem Levi was very opposed to this idea of treating the rich differently than the poor. He was a compassionate man who refused to judge the worth of a man's life by his financial state. So Dr. Levi often treated patients who could not afford medical help and he became known for this willingness to give care to those in need. His kind heart was appreciated by all who were sick and in need. However, long days at his medical office left him overworked and exhausted. Although he could have lived with all the comforts of a wealthy man if had he chosen to work for the rich, Levi and his family lived a simple life. The Levis had a roof over their heads, practical furniture, and food in their bellies. But what impressed Dovid most about his father was that the Levis had a kind, fair but stubborn man as the head of their household.

Dr. Levi wanted to shelter his son from how worried he was about the Nazis invading Russia. However, the truth could not be kept from Dovid. He knew what was going on in the world even before he listened to his parents talking that night. Dovid heard people jabbering about the Nazis in the streets. His friends at school discussed the future of Russia with fear in their voices. And although his father had tried to hide the truth, Dovid knew that the Germans had invaded the Soviet Union and were headed towards Kiev. Every day his father seemed to grow more and more on edge. Seeing his father's hands shake and his eye twitch was frightening to Dovid because Levi had never been this way. In the past, he'd always been a calm man whose profession had forced him to make life and death decisions every day.

Dovid pressed his ear against the wall and continued to listen.

"Raisa, I am worried. I know things have not been good for us Jews here in Russia under Stalin, but who knows what Hitler will bring? It could be worse."

"Maybe it will be better for us," Raisa said. "Stalin has starved the country. The Russian people have endured a terrible famine under his rule. And God help us if we even say one word against this government and how they are handling our lives. Perhaps the Nazis will not be as harsh."

"Maybe. We can only hope. But I don't count on it. We are Jews. The world hates us and you and I both know that things never get better for us Jews. We are always in danger. I wish we had a country of our own. But I suppose that has been the dream of every Jew since the beginning of time. Nu, Raisa?"

"Yes, of course. I would love to have a safe place where we could raise Dovid without worry."

"They call us the chosen people. But since the beginning of time Jews have faced a world filled with hatred. No matter where we live, our people are always at risk for a pogrom. And I am terribly afraid that we are at risk now. I don't care for myself but I worry for the safety of you my dear wife, and our son, our Dovid. You see, Raisa, any kind of change in the government makes me nervous."

"You think the Germans will take Kiev?"

"I have every reason to believe that they will." Menachem cleared his throat. "That Hitler is a ruthless bastard."

"Eh, so Stalin isn't?"

"Yes, of course he is. Two bad eggs they are. I wish we could send Dovid away. I wish we could send him somewhere where he would be safe when the Nazis come, just in case there is trouble."

"But where? We have no place to send him."

"He has an uncle, my brother, in the United States."

"How can we arrange for him to go there now? It is too late. The Germans should be at the borders of Kiev within days. Besides, Menachem, you give away your medical services so often that we hardly have enough money to live. Where would we get the money for his passage to America?"

"I have money hidden."

"You surprise me, Menny. You hid it from me?"

She only called him Menny when they were alone in their room, Dovid thought.

It was like her secret pet name for him. It was hard for Dovid to see his parents as lovers, but when he heard them talking alone in their room at night he saw a side of them that they never showed him during the day.

"Not from you, my Raisa. My darling, my love. Everything I have is yours. But every time I could I put a little bit away in case of an emergency. I have been doing this for my entire life. Someday, when I am dead, you will be glad to have a little savings."

"Stop it, Menny. I don't want to think about you dying. That's bad luck. Poo, poo, poo."

Dovid knew she was spitting on his father to ward off the evil spirits.

"My sweet, superstitious Raisa, I do love you so much."

"Oh Menny, if only I had known about the money. We could have gotten Dovid out of here. But it's too late now."

"So what should we do?" Menachem said not really asking Raisa, more just voicing the question to himself.

"The cellar, I suppose? Perhaps we must hide him in the cellar when the Nazis come," Raisa said.

"We'll see. I have to think this through. I don't know what we are going to do yet," Menachem said.

Dovid felt a bolt of fear travel like lightning through his spine.

Hide in the cellar? For how long? Is this going to be a pogrom like the ones I heard my parents talk about where invading armies of angry men come through our town and kill Jews for no reason? Maybe Mama is right about the Nazis. I pray she is. Maybe the Germans will be better for us Jews than the Russians have been.

It was early September and although it was cool outside, Dovid could feel the sweat beading on his forehead. His parents had stopped talking. Dovid heard his mother moan softly. He wondered if his father was kissing her. The thought was not one he chose to entertain. So Dovid lay back down on his bed. His heart was still pounding. He knew he should get some rest, he had to get up early for school. But Dovid could not sleep at all that night.

CHAPTER SIX

✡

The first thirteen years of Dovid Levi's life had been fairly calm and sheltered. He had been an only child, doted upon by his parents. However, all of that was about to change. The nightmare that he would come to call his existence began in the wee hours of a cool September morning in 1941. He'd been asleep, dreaming a sweet dream about the dog he'd been begging his father to let him bring home. A friend from school had a mutt that had given birth to three mangy puppies a few weeks earlier. When Dovid saw the puppies he immediately fell in love with the smallest one—a brown and white female. He picked her up and she nuzzled his hand. From that moment he knew he had to find a way to talk his father into letting him bring her home.

Now, in his dream, she was his. They were playing fetch with a stick. Dovid smiled in his sleep. But then German planes roared overhead. There was a series of terrible loud crashes as bombs rained down on the city. Dovid awakened to the pounding of blood behind his temples. His mouth was dry as he got up and ran into his parents' room. His mother was sitting up in bed, disoriented. Her hair was askew, and a look of panic covered her delicate features. His father snapped into control quickly.

"Get down on the floor, hurry, Dovid, Raisa. On the floor now. Cover your heads."

Dovid stubbed his toe on the bedpost as he jumped down to follow his father's orders. His entire foot throbbed with pain as his mother held him close to her. He looked up and saw that she was crying.

The Levis lay on the floor listening to the neighboring houses explode. As the sound of each bomb blast filled the air, they prayed that their home would not be next.

Then on September 19th the German soldiers entered Kiev. Some came in tanks that looked like giant moving fortresses, others came proudly goose-stepping through the village wearing their swastika armbands. A large group of Nazis settled in the center of town. It was then that they raised their flag. The German soldiers rejoiced as they tore down posters of Stalin and replaced them with pictures of their leader Adolf Hitler.

At first, the Germans were kind to the people of Kiev, promising that the Reich would bring better leadership than the Bolsheviks. They moved into buildings in the center of town and spent time talking to the Russian citizens, encouraging them to rally against Stalin's rule.

But then the buildings where the Germans had taken up residence were bombed. There was death and destruction everywhere. Pools of thick dark red blood stained the streets. Dovid had never witnessed such horror. He ran to his father's office after school only to find both parents waiting for him. His mother immediately went to him like he was a child and took him into her arms. In the past he would have protested her treating him like a little boy because he was thirteen and had already had his bah-mitzvah. But when he looked into her eyes he saw the anguish and he felt like a child again, longing to be safe in her bosom.

The bombings continued for almost two weeks. Whenever a bomb landed close by there was a deafening roar, and the smell of smoke was ever present in the air. Another doctor would have closed his practice and stayed at home with his family but not Dr. Levi. He knew that people needed his services, and even more so now that there were so many being injured in the streets. And so Dr. Levi packed his black medicine bag each morning and went off to work in the midst of an Armageddon in the streets.

CHAPTER SEVEN

✡

**Ukraine under Nazi occupation
The end of September 1941**

Maria Ivanov knew what it meant to live a hard life. She'd been the daughter of a farmer then the wife of one, Stas Ivanov. She and Stas had gotten out of bed before sunrise every morning to tend the land. There were no days off, no holidays, and no time to be sick. When she was pregnant she worked on the farm all the way up until she went into labor. Then she stopped to give birth to the two boys but the following day she was up and working again. The boys were twins but not identical in either looks or personality.

Maria never expected more out of life than she got as the wife of a farmer. She knew that her life with Stas would not be glamorous and that they would always struggle to make ends meet. It was a well-known fact that, being people of the land, farmers walked a tightrope dependent upon the whims of the weather for their daily bread.

Her husband had never been tender. He'd always been a difficult man. Most times he was cold and distant towards her but she knew that was just his way. Maria believed that Stas loved her but he just didn't realize it. However, most of all, she knew that she loved him. So she catered to him and accepted him as he was.

When the government confiscated the Ivanov's land in order to create kolkhozes—collective farms where all of their land and animals would be owned by the government—Stas resisted. They would no longer be allowed to sell any excess grain. Instead, the government would take all of their produce and pay them back with a small amount of goods. She'd begged him not to try and fight against Stalin's iron fist. But he was not willing to give up the land that had been in his family for generations. Stas fought back and was arrested. He was sent to a gulag in

Siberia.

A year later she received a letter informing her that her husband was dead. That was all the information that the letter gave her concerning his demise but she'd heard enough about the gulags to know that he'd been worked hard and starved. Very few people ever left the prisons alive. And so the government had its way. It took the land and all Stas accomplished by fighting was his own death.

Now two years after she received the letter telling her Stas was dead, Maria and her two sons lived on just an acre that was part of a collective farm. She and her boys were required to work until they reached their productivity quota, which was high. In order to meet it, they worked from sun up to sun down. All of the farmers in the collective knew that if they were unable to satisfy the government's demands the threat of prison hung over their heads.

An acre of land was hardly enough to grow everything that was required, and most of the grain they produced was confiscated by the government, leaving little for the family to live on. The twin boys, thirteen years old and growing, were always hungry. Some of their neighbors tried to hide grain by burying it but after losing her husband Maria Ivanov was not willing to risk losing her sons. A single cow was all that was left to them; the government took the rest of their animals. From that cow they produced milk and cheese, most of which also had to be turned over to the government. But at least they had some milk, some cheese, and a little grain. Even though they received no money for their work and they only got a very small part of all they produced, Maria had learned early in life to be grateful for whatever crumbs were thrown to her. Many nights she sacrificed her evening meal, giving it to her sons so that they would not go to bed hungry.

Ivan grew up to be a friendly and outgrowing boy but Oskar was more introverted. He was cold and distant, especially to strangers. Maria could see Stas' personality in Oskar but she saw herself in Ivan. Oskar didn't make friends easily. In fact, the only people he ever spoke to were his brother and his mother. The boys never went to school; there was too much work on a farm to spare them for any length of time. Ivan would have liked to have gone, but Oskar was glad to not have to interact with others.

It was a September morning, past sunrise, when Maria noticed that Oskar was not outside working. She told Ivan she would be right back and went quickly up to the house. Oskar had never gotten out of bed that morning. He was still curled up on the floor in his bed of straw.

He has to be very ill, Maria thought, her brow knitted with worry. Oskar was not lazy and he was not one to sleep late, either. He and Ivan always awakened at the crack of dawn and were out working the land. Most days they were both out earlier than their mother. Even when the boys were little they had done their part. The previous night both boys had complained of stomachaches. This was not the first time any of the Ivanovs had felt under the weather but normally they went to work anyway. Maria was worried. Everyone in the family knew how important it was for them to carry their own load.

Ivan was fully recovered from his stomachache by the morning and was up and out working. Oskar, however, seemed to have gotten worse. Several times during the night he had to run out of the mud hut where they lived due to bloody diarrhea, and he was vomiting profusely.

"Stay in bed, Oskar. We'll manage. Don't worry. You'll feel better by tonight," Maria whispered to her son.

"I'm so sorry, Mama. I can't move. I feel terrible."

"I know. It's all right. Rest."

"But the work. There is so much work," Oskar said.

"Shh. Rest. We will take care of everything, Ivan and I." She leaned down and kissed his cheek and then went out to farm the land.

Three days passed and still Oskar did not get any better. In fact, when Maria and Ivan came into the house to have their afternoon meal they found him listless to the point of unresponsive.

Maria couldn't eat her bread and soup even though her stomach was growling with hunger. She picked up her bowl and went over to Oskar. Her hand was trembling as she tried to feed him.

"Oskar. It's me, Mama. Oskar, wake up please." But he did not open his eyes. He lay on his bed of straw in the corner. The smell surrounding him was so strong that it made Maria gag. Then she broke down in tears. "I'm afraid he's dead."

"Check his pulse," Ivan said.

"I can't." She was weeping.

Ivan walked over and put his hand on his twin brother's neck. It was like looking at himself in death. But then he felt a pulse. "He's alive, Mama."

"Oh praise God!" Maria said. "I have to help

him somehow. I am so worried."

"I know, so am I," Ivan said.

"I refuse to take him to the people's hospital," Maria said shaking her head.

"We'll figure this out. For now, you must eat Mama; please, you must eat. You have been working very hard."

She could not eat. Her soup was sitting in front of her getting cold. "If I take him to that hospital he will die there for sure."

"Yes, I agree with you. I would rather keep him at home than take him there. I visited a friend there once who was sick. It was a terrible place. Frightening. As I walked through the hallways I heard screaming coming from the rooms. And everyone knows that the nurses and orderlies never come into the patients' rooms to see what is wrong. They don't care. Unless the patient's family can give them bribes, they just let the poor soul die."

Maria nodded her head. This was common knowledge. She would never take her precious son to that place. Never. If he were going to die, then he'd die at home with people who loved him. Maria bit her lip. Just the thought of her son Oskar dying brought more tears. She had to think of something. And then ….

Maria knew of only one doctor in Kiev who would see her son without payment. She'd never met him but she'd heard others say how kind he was to the poor. It was Levi, the Jew. He gave them credit and told them to pay when they were able. Levi never turned anyone away who needed help. Never! Not even people whom he knew would never return to settle their debt.

"I am going to take Oskar into town to see Levi, the Jew," Mrs. Ivanov said to Ivan. "He needs a doctor badly. I believe that the Jew will see him without money. At least that's what everyone says. And we have no money to pay…"

Ivan nodded. "Would you like me to go with you? There are Nazis in Kiev. It's not safe for a woman and a sick boy without anyone to defend them."

"No, Ivan, you must stay here. I am a grown woman. I will be fine. You watch the farm."

Ivan went next door and begged the neighbor to borrow his horse. "My brother is very sick," he told the neighbor. "If my mother doesn't get him to a doctor quickly he will die."

The neighbor screwed up his face. "I don't like to send my horse out for no reason."

"I'm begging you. Please. We need your help. When I was seven and you were sick, my Papa came and helped you with your farming. Do you remember? He is dead now. We are two boys and a woman alone, badly in need of your horse. You can't refuse us. Please."

The neighbor dropped his shoulders and looked at Ivan. "You're right. Your father was a big help to me. I can still remember how much he did for my family." The neighbor took a deep breath and sighed. "The horse is in the barn. Take him. Your mother will need to use my cart. It's in the barn as well."

"I will never be able to thank you enough."

"Go now."

Ivan led the horse out of his stall and saddled him to the cart. Then he rode the cart back to his house. Maria helped Ivan carry Oskar out to the cart and gently placed him into his seat. Maria took the reins as the old horse whinnied. Ivan kissed his mother's cheek goodbye as Maria began the drive into Kiev.

Maria Ivanov lived a secluded life on her farm located several miles outside of town. The only people she ever had contact with were her neighbors, other families in the farming collective, and the Russian soldiers who came to collect the produce they were required to give to the government.

When she arrived in Kiev Maria was shocked. She was immediately confronted with pools of dried blood, dead bodies on the streets, and buildings that were completely reduced to nothing but rubble from the onslaught of bombs. Her son had warned her that there were Nazis in Kiev but she wasn't expecting this! She swallowed hard and straightened the kerchief she wore around her head.

There is no turning back now. I must do what I can to help my son, she thought.

With a quick whip to the horse, Maria made her way to the Jewish sector of town. There she found the gray stone building that she'd heard so many people describe. There was a sign above the storefront in black letters. If Maria had been taught to read she would have known that the sign said:

" Levi, Physician."

She looked in the window to be sure she was in the right place. But all she saw was a staircase leading to a second floor.

I am fairly sure that this is it. At least I hope I am right, she thought. Then a man came walking quickly by. "Do you know if this is the office of Dr. Levi?"

"It says so right there on the sign," the man said, pulling his coat tighter around his neck against the chill of the night wind.

Oskar was weak and unable to stand on his own, but that didn't deter her. Maria lifted her son in her arms. Years of tilling the soil had made her strong. She carried Oskar into the building and then, although she was strained and out of breath, she continued up the narrow staircase to the doctor's office. The waiting room was filled with people but when the doctor peeked his head out the door to call the next patient, he took one look at Oskar and told Maria to bring him into the office immediately.

Dovid Levi, the doctor's only child, took Ivan's arm and helped Maria to place him on the examining table.

"What is your name?" the doctor asked, looking directly into Oskar's eyes.

At first, the boy didn't answer. He looked at the doctor. His eyes were glassy and bloodshot and he seemed confused. Again the doctor asked Oskar in a clear voice, "Your name son, what is your name?" Dr. Levi shook the boy. Then he held Oskar's head until Oskar's eyes focused on him.

"Oskar Ivanov."

"How old are you, Oskar?"

"I am about to turn 14 next month," Oskar croaked.

"You're almost the same age as my son, my Dovid. Dovid is 13 but he won't be 14 for several months," the doctor said, smiling.

Oskar tried to smile back but as his dry and crusty lips turned upward his eyes fluttered closed and he lost consciousness.

Dr. Levi examined the boy thoroughly. Then he took Maria by the arm and led her out of the room to speak to her.

"Your son is very ill. Did he drink milk fresh from a cow or goat recently?"

She nodded. "We have an acre of land as part of a collective farm. Do you know where the farms are? They are outside the city?"

"I have passed them. I am sure I have seen yours. But you must have come a long way into the city?" he asked, trying to make casual conversation in order to help her calm down a little while he asked her some important questions.

Maria went on to explain where the Ivanov farm was located. "We have one cow. I believe that Oskar milked her the day he got sick. He could have drunk some of the milk."

"Do you pasteurize your milk?"

" I don't know what you mean by pasteurize."

"Never mind then. I am going to assume that he drank milk that was straight from the cow," the doctor said. Dr. Levi was pretty sure that the boy was dying.

How can I find a way to tell a mother that her son is dying?

"Will he be all right? Can you help him?"

"I can't promise you anything, " Dr. Levi murmured, his voice soft with sympathy. "But I'll do everything I can for him. Leave him here with me. I will stay at the office with him and take care of him through the night."

"I can't afford to pay you, Doctor. I don't

have any money and since the Nazis invaded the country has taken even more of what we produce on the farm for the war effort. There is hardly enough left for us to eat. You see, Doctor, I am a widow. My parents are dead and my siblings live far away. All I have left in the world are my twin boys…"

Dr. Levi sighed. He'd heard that story more often than he could remember. But he couldn't turn this boy away; his conscience wouldn't let him.

"Don't worry about payment right now. You can pay me when you are able. The best thing for you to do right now is to leave the boy here. He is very sick and, as I said, I can't make promises. But you have my word that I will try my best. After all, I understand how you feel Mrs. Ivanov. I, too, have a son," Dr. Levi said and glanced over at Dovid.

"May God bless you, Doctor. Please do your best for him." Maria had tears in her eyes. "I don't know how I can go on without him."

"Well, let's not think about that right now. Let's do what we can for him," Dr. Levi said,

63

touching Oskar's forehead gently. The boy was burning up. Menachem Levi felt a shiver run down his spine. He said a silent prayer in Hebrew then he turned to the mother again and said, "Be careful on your way home. The streets are dangerous."

"I will," she said and left.

CHAPTER EIGHT

✡

Despite all of the good doctor's efforts of bathing the boy in alcohol to bring down his fever and staying with him constantly, Oskar Ivanov did not make it through the night. It was as Dr. Levi feared. The boy had contracted a rare disease from the raw milk that shut his kidneys down.

Levi felt the weight of the world on his shoulders. He had done everything in his power to try and save the boy, but in the end, it was God's will that the child go home to him. Even when he was just a student of medicine, Levi always took it hard when he lost a patient, but to lose such a young boy was the most heartbreaking of all. A young man, with so much ahead of him, gone in an instant.

And there is nothing I can do, Dr. Levi thought.

"Dovid, you are exhausted. I'll walk you home so you'll be safe."

"I can go alone," Dovid said.

"Yes, I am sure you can, son. But I'll go with you," his father said.

They walked silently. When they got home, Dr. Levi said," You get some rest now, Dovid, and stay inside."

The doctor walked slowly back to his office. His shoulders were hunched in defeat. How could he lay his head down on his pillow and rest? The boy was dead. He'd failed the poor widow Ivanov. The least Levi could do was not leave the body alone inside the dark, cold, empty office. He would stay with him through the night. He turned the key in the lock and opened the door to his office building. An eerie silence greeted him; the only sound was the click of his heels as he walked up to the table where the body of Oskar Ivanov lay still and peaceful in death. Menachem wept as he looked into the face of the young man, not just because Oskar was dead but because Oskar Ivanov bore an uncanny resemblance to his own Dovid. A chill ran up Menachem Levi's spine. What if this was Dovid laying there lifeless? Dr. Levi spit three times to ward off the evil spirits. Then he covered the body with a blanket. Intellectually, he knew that a dead child wouldn't feel the cold, but somehow it made the doctor feel better to see Oskar's body covered with a blanket instead of just a sheet.

Tomorrow I will have to tell his poor mother that I was unsuccessful. Then she will leave my office with a dead body instead of a healthy young son, he grieved.

The following day the widow and her son Ivan returned to the doctor's office to check on Oskar.

"Please, sit down," Dr. Levi said, indicating toward two chairs in his office. He hesitated. "I'm sorry. I tried everything, but I couldn't save him. Oskar has passed away." Dr. Levi threw his arms up in surrender

The widow stared at the doctor in disbelief. Young Ivan's face turned to chalk as he trembled at his mother's side but he did not speak. A painful silence filled the room. For several moments no one spoke. Then the widow's face crumbled and the doctor held her while she wept.

"If there is anything I can do for you, please let me know," Dr. Levi said.

"What do we owe you, Doctor?" Ivan asked. "I can't pay you now, but I will take on extra work to pay off our bill."

"Nothing. You owe me nothing." Dr. Levi patted Ivan's shoulder. "Take care of your mother. She needs you now," he added.

Levi helped the boy carry Oskar's body out to the cart while Maria walked beside them. Depression and a feeling of loss lingered over the doctor for the rest of the day.

After Dr. Levi finished with all the patients in his waiting room he packed the black leather bag that he took home with him each night in case someone came to him with an emergency. Then he locked the office. He was glad to be heading home. It would be nice to take a warm bath and have something to eat.

On his way, he passed a brick building with a large maple tree beside it. It was the same red brick building and tree he had passed every morning and evening for years but today a new sign had been nailed to the side of the tree. It was placed at reading level where it could not be missed. The doctor was sure that it had not been there that morning. Even though he longed for the relief going home would give him on that terrible day, he took a few minutes to stop and read it.

It said: All Jews living in Kiev must report for resettlement. The Jews are responsible for the bombing of the buildings where the Nazis settled. It is mandatory that anyone of Jewish descent be at the corner of Melnikovsky and Dokhturov streets next to the cemetery by 8 a.m. on Monday, the 29th of September 1941. All Jews must bring with them any important documents, valuables, warm clothes, underclothes, and money. Anyone who fails to follow these instructions will be shot on sight.

Doctor Levi put his bag on the ground and reread the notice.

He knew that the Nazis had taken Kiev and had settled into various buildings throughout the city. He also knew that there had recently been a bombing of the buildings where the Nazis were living. Now they were blaming the Jews.

A possible resettlement? Where? This could turn out to be an imprisonment.

I am not surprised that the Germans are blaming us. This idea of blaming the Jews for everything that goes wrong is nothing new. The Russians have been doing it for centuries. My poor Raisa. I know that she is hopeful that the Germans will be better than the Russians have been. The Communists were supposed to be better than the white Russians and they weren't. I doubt the Nazis are going to be any better than all the others.

But the very idea of a resettlement has me on edge. Hashem, please, protect our people. They could very well be sending us to something similar to a gulag. Oy, my Raisa and my Dovid in a gulag! How can I protect them there? I know the Germans are in control of us and we must follow their orders or they will kill us for certain. But I feel very uneasy about them. Very uneasy. Perhaps in many ways, I am more fearful of them than I am of the Russians.

I wish I could find a way to leave Dovid here in Kiev in hiding until I have a better idea of what the Germans have in store for us. Then once Raisa and I are settled, if it is at all possible, we would do what we could to make the best of things. If we are not in a gulag in Siberia, I would send for Dovid.

But who can I turn to for something so perilous? We are Jews. No one in his right mind would risk his life to save a Jew. Even so, I must think of someone who would be willing to put himself in terrible danger in order to help us protect Dovid.

CHAPTER NINE

✡

After Dovid went to bed that night, Menachem and Raisa discussed the notice. Menachem was not surprised to find that although his wife couldn't read, she already knew all about the notice. The whole neighborhood was buzzing with the news. Raisa was trembling when she told her husband that they must report on Monday for resettlement.

"Everyone is talking about this. Menachem, I don't want to leave my home, all of our friends, our shul, the things we've worked so hard for. Some of these things could never be replaced. They have sentimental value. My Bubbe's dishes. They were in our family for generations. And how about my mother's dining table?" she whimpered.

"I know, Raisa. I know. But the house and the material things are the least of our worries. They are only things. I am worried about our family. I don't know what they are planning to do with us."

"Do you think they are going to send us to Siberia?"

"I don't know. I am not sure what they are going to do."

"Oh, I am scared. You're right. Our things don't mean anything. You, Dovid. That is what is important. Our lives…" Her voice had gotten loud and shrill.

"Shhh. You'll wake Dovid. Right now we don't know anything for sure. So please calm down," he said, hugging her shoulder. "Now I want to talk to you about something; I have an idea. I don't think we should take Dovid with us if we can help it. We know where we are going. I want to do what we can to keep him safe. Do you agree?"

Raisa shrugged her shoulders. She was crying softly.

Menachem went on. "Anyway, there is a woman who lives on a farm on the outskirts of the city. She came to see me yesterday. Her son was very sick. I treated him but unfortunately, he died. The boy was the same age as Dovid. The woman is a widow and I am sure she will probably need help on the farm. I can't say for certain that she will be willing, but tomorrow I am going to drive out to her farm and see her. She might not be willing but I am going to ask her to take Dovid into her home and keep him until I can send for him. I know this sounds farfetched, but perhaps Dovid can pose as her son. They looked a great deal alike…"

"Are you crazy? Menachem, our son should be with his parents, not staying on a farm with a non-Jewish woman and her son. What are you thinking?"

"I am thinking that if by some miracle this woman will agree, our Dovid will be safe until we can send for him."

They argued through the night. Raisa wept. She pled with her husband to reconsider. But in the end, Menachem refused to back down. In the morning he woke Dovid and told him to get dressed. Then Levi put his arm around his precious son, bent down, and kissed him. "Kiss your mother, Dovid. You are going away for a while," he said.

Dovid looked at his father in disbelief. But he kissed his mother. "Papa, where am I going?"

"Come, Dovid. You must trust me. Do as I tell you," Menachem said.

Menachem took Dovid for a long ride. They drove until they were out of the city and the land rolled out before them with open fields, farms, horses, and cows. They continued their journey until they arrived at a farm with a white wood-framed house. Menachem eased the car onto the dirt road, then he parked and got out. He motioned for Dovid to follow him. Menachem saw Dovid from the corner of his eye Once Dovid stood beside him, Menachem knocked on the door of the farmhouse owned by the widow Ivanov.

"Where are we, Papa?" Dovid asked.

His father looked directly at Dovid and then quickly embraced his son.

Menachem Levi gripped onto Dovid's jacket and held him tight. At that moment he thought that he knew what Abraham must have felt when he took his son Isaac up the mountain to sacrifice his son to God.

Hashem, please have mercy on me and spare my child as you spared Isaac for Abraham. Please save my Dovid, he prayed.

When the widow opened the door her face was red from crying. Her eyes were deep and dark and Menachem could see the pain radiating out of them.

How can I come here to her house to ask this of her today? And yet, I must. If she will agree, this farm will be a safe haven for Dovid until Raisa and I can send for him.

"Mrs. Ivanov."

"Come in, Doctor Levi," she said opening the door to the farmhouse.

Levi and his son entered the sparsely furnished living area.

"Please, won't you sit down."

Dr. Levi sat and nodded his head to Dovid indicating that he may do the same.

"Mrs. Ivanov. I am sorry to come to your home and bother you during your hour of grief. I am not usually one to ask for the return of a favor. However, today I must. You see… on this coming Monday, all of the Jews in Kiev are being rounded up for relocation. As you know, I am Jewish. And, quite frankly, I'm very worried about where they might send us. Until we are safe and settled somewhere …" He hesitated and cleared his throat. "Until we are settled my wife and I…." Levi coughed.

"Go on…" Maria said.

"I don't even know how to say this. So, I will just say it. Mrs. Ivanov, I have come to ask you if Dovid could stay with you here on the farm where he would be safe until my wife and I can send for him. He could pose as your son Oskar. They look very much alike."

"Oh doctor, I don't know about this…"

"But you are certainly going to need another hand to help you with the farm. With Oskar gone, may he rest in peace, all of Oskar's work will fall upon Ivan's shoulders. Perhaps having Dovid's help would be a blessing to you. He is strong. He could help you."

Maria looked at Ivan then she frowned at Dr. Levi. "I'm not sure this is such a good idea. If we are caught…"

"Mrs. Ivanov. My son is in danger. Please. I am begging you to help us. Besides, I also have money. I will give you money." The doctor's hands were trembling as he pulled out a small wallet filled with cash.

Maria glanced at Ivan who stood in the corner of the room. "What do you think?" she asked him.

"I will need help with the farm. And we can use the money," Ivan said. "The boy is a Jew and because of that, I am not sure if we can trust him. Jews can be underhanded. But still, Mama, there is a lot of work to be done to keep this farm running. You are working so hard now that I can't expect much more from you. Oskar and I were the strong ones. Now all the heavy work will fall to me."

"Do you think anyone will recognize that it is not Oskar?"

"I don't believe they will. Oskar never talked to anyone. He kept to himself. This boy looks enough like him that I don't think anyone will be the wiser."

"Please. I am begging you." Menachem Levi took a roll of bills out of his wallet and laid them on the table. Ivan and the widow stared at the money. The doctor continued, "I will send for my son as soon as I can. I am not sure of what the next few days will bring and I want to know that, no matter what happens, Dovid is here with you ... safe. Please ..."

"He could pass for Oskar. And we don't have any real friends who would notice or care. All of our relatives are far away. Who would even know the difference? We hardly ever see anyone. Once in a while we wave to a neighbor. But everyone is so busy with their own quotas that we hardly ever speak. So, it is safe to say that people would easily think that this boy was Oskar," Ivan said.

"What about when the boy leaves us to go

back to his parents?" the widow asked her son.

"Then we can have a funeral and tell the neighbors, if anyone should ask, that Oskar died."

The widow thought for a moment. "Well, we certainly could use the help. And the money."

"Yes, Mother, we could," Ivan said.

Levi stood in front of the cash trembling…waiting. The next few minutes would determine the safety of his precious boy. He refused to look over at Dovid who was trying to get his father's attention.

"He is an attractive boy. He doesn't look like a Jew, does he?" Maria asked Ivan.

"No, Mother. He reminds me of my Oskar."

"And you did help me when I was in need and asked nothing in return," Maria said.

"So …what do you say?" the doctor asked, his palms were sweating.

Dovid walked over to his father and

grabbed his shoulders. "Papa, you want to leave me here? Why? Where are you and Mama going? What is all this talk about resettlement?"

"The Nazis have taken over Kiev. They are rounding up all of the Jews. I don't know where they are sending us. It's a resettlement. Once we are settled we will send for you."

"A resettlement? This is our home, Papa. This has always been our home."

"I know, Dovid. But we must do what they ask."

"Why? Why must we do what they ask?"

"Because I am your father and I know what is best," Levi said. His eyes were determined but filled with unshed tears.

"I want to go with you and Mama. Please, Papa, don't leave me here with strangers. Wherever they send you, that is where I want to be too."

"Hush, Dovid. If these kind people will take you into their home, the Levis will be forever grateful."

Dovid knew his father and he knew that he must not say another word. Once his father made up his mind about something it was settled. There was nothing to discuss.

"So …again, I am pleading with you…can he stay, Mrs. Ivanov?" This was hard for him. He had never begged anyone for anything before in his life. And, had it not been that he was so concerned for the safety of his son, he would not be begging now. He would have accepted his fate, whatever it might be. But not his Dovid. His boy must be protected, no matter what he had to sacrifice—money, pride. Nothing mattered … only Dovid.

"Yes. It's all right with me if he stays here for a while," Maria said. She turned to Ivan. "What do you say?"

"I say yes," Ivan answered. He looked relieved to have someone to help him with all the heavy farm work. "Tonight, when no one can see us, you will help me bury my brother," Ivan said to Dovid. "And from then on, you will be known as Oskar Ivanov."

"Thank you," Menachem Levi said and

turned to go.

"Papa," Dovid ran into his father's arms. Menachem held his son tightly for several moments. His heart ached as it never had before. He kissed the top of Dovid's head. "I love you, my son," he said. Then he turned and walked out of the house.

CHAPTER TEN

✡

When Menachem was alone in his car driving back to his home in Kiev, he let the tears fall. He had no idea when or if he would see his son again.

This is the hardest thing I've ever done. I've been through the death of my parents. The loss of a sibling. My Raisa had a miscarriage in her eighth month. I've seen illness and death but nothing has been as difficult as leaving my son behind.

When Menachem returned home from dropping Dovid off at the Ivanov's farm, Raisa would not speak to him. His heart was heavy and he was in no mood to try and comfort his wife. There would be patients waiting at his medical office, but he could not find the energy to go in and treat them. He was conflicted. For some reason, he felt that he'd made the right decision in leaving Dovid at the farm. But he couldn't be sure. Little pangs of doubt crept into his mind and he began to worry again. In fact, he began to realize that he wasn't sure of anything. The Soviets under Stalin had tolerated but openly hated the Jews. However, he had been frightened by the reaction of the Nazis to the bombing of their homes. Their first reaction was to strike out at the Jews. This action was far too reminiscent of the pogroms that had occurred for years in the Soviet Union back when it was still known as Russia. The Jews were on the chopping block again.

We are losing our homes and all our material goods. My practice is being uprooted. But I don't care about the material things.

He knew as a doctor he would always have work and his practice would rebuild wherever they were sent. But Dovid? Have I done what is best for Dovid? It was hard not to second-guess his decision. If they were headed to some prison in Siberia would it be better for Dovid if they took him with them? There was always a chance they would be subjected to starvation and the weather in Siberia was anything but welcoming. At least on a farm

Dovid would have food and warmth. Then who knows? Perhaps the Soviets would defeat the Nazis and the Levis could return to Kiev. Or maybe the relocation would not be terrible and he would feel comfortable bringing Dovid to live with them. His mind was racing. He wished he had a crystal ball to help him know if he'd made the right choice.

Menachem was quiet. He was still conflicted as he and his wife packed everything they owned of value before sunrise on that Monday morning.

They left the house at seven in the morning. Both he and Raisa were carrying suitcases filled with their lives. They'd packed the necessities but they'd both also slipped in a few pictures of their parents, of Dovid, of the day they were married.

Menachem saw that the suitcase was too heavy for his delicate wife and so he took it from her and carried both as they followed the rest of their neighbors, also on their way to report.

"Where is Dovid?" Mrs. Sachovich, a

woman who lived down the street asked Raisa.

"He left earlier with some of his friends."

"Smart boy," Mrs. Sachovich said. " We should have left earlier. There will probably only be standing room left on the train by the time we can board."

"You are probably right. I can't believe how many people are gathered here," Raisa said as they got in at the end of the line outside the cemetery. The two women had been friends for several years. Now as they waited in line, both of them wanting to ask the same question, but neither of them daring to do so: "Where are they sending us?"

CHAPTER ELEVEN

✡

Dovid Levi helped Ivan bury his brother Oskar by the light of a full moon that same night. But even as he dug the grave, Dovid knew that he was not going to stay at the farm. He was going to find his parents and follow them. There was no doubt that his father would be furious. The best thing to do was hide in the back of the cemetery and watch as the rest of his Jewish neighbors boarded the train. Once they were all on board, Dovid would sneak in at the end of the line. After the train reached its destination, Dovid planned to find his parents. By then it would be too late for his father to insist he return.

Ivan and his mother were kind enough to Dovid. He couldn't complain, but Dovid wanted to be with his own family. So on the morning of September 29, he got up at 3 a.m. and while Maria and Ivan slept, Dovid quietly left the farmhouse. He walked for several miles and climbed the back fence of the cemetery. By the time he arrived, he could see lines already forming. He knew some of the people from his neighborhood and others from his father's practice. They were all Jewish. He recognized Devorah, the girl who lived three streets away from him. He'd had a secret crush on her since last year when they were both at the market and she had smiled at him. Now she stood beside her parents, holding the hand of a younger sister. In front of them was a pile of suitcases. Why had her parents been willing to take their children, but Dovid's papa been so adamant about leaving him behind?

It is a good thing that I played with my friends in this very cemetery when I was a child because I can still remember this unknown opening in the wall, he thought, easily slipping through the hole. *And now that I am inside, I know all of the good places to hide.*

Dovid found a spot where he could watch the Jews where no one could see him.

He sat back, watching and thinking.

By the time my parents arrive at their destination, they will be forced to accept that I am there with them. My father will be mad, but at least I will be with my family. But just to be safe and sure that my father doesn't see me I have to be the last person to get on the train.

At precisely eight that morning, the Germans arrived, looking powerful in their belted uniforms, guns at their sides. They began barking orders in a mixture of Russian and German. They spoke enough Russian for Dovid to make out what they wanted.

"Leave your luggage at the front of the line. It will be delivered to you in a van," the Nazis said.

Dovid watched as the Nazis controlled the crowd. Only a few people were allowed to move forward at a time. In the distance, he heard a tic, tic, tic sound.

What is that? Where is there a train?

Dovid waited to move forward until he saw his mother and father. He continued to hide and watch as they moved forward. He assumed they were in line with the rest of the group to board a waiting train. But where?

However, once Dovid's parents got to the front of the line Dovid saw that there was no train. In fact, he saw a row of Nazis with their guns drawn and pointed at the Jews. The Germans were hollering loud enough for him to understand.

"Present your identification papers," they said.

"Jude!" One of the Germans yelled as he pushed Dovid's father forward. Another checked his mother's papers and announced "Jude," shoving her until she almost fell.

Dovid felt a shroud of dread come over him.

Ten people were counted out before the line was stopped.

Dovid continued to follow in the shadows. He was so close that the Nazis could have grabbed him but they couldn't see him. He watched in helpless terror as his parents were forced through a line that had been created by guards with thick wooden sticks on each side. The guards were bashing the Jews with their weapons and yelling "Schnell, faster! Move faster!"

Dovid saw that his father's cheek was bleeding and his mother was in tears. He wanted to jump out and start fighting the soldiers, but he was too afraid. His cowardice at that moment would haunt him for the rest of his days on earth. However, as much as he longed to defend his loved ones, his feet stayed glued to the ground until his parents moved through the end of the manmade hall of horror. There they were forced to take off all of their clothes. His mother, always so modest, refused. She was weeping, pleading. One of the soldiers laughed and hit her across the shoulder with a club. Slender and delicate, she fell to the ground. Dovid's father helped her up only to be clubbed for his efforts.

Dovid felt vomit rise in his throat. Mama, Papa…

"Get undressed right now!" The guard's face was red as he screamed his order at Raisa

Levi.

This time she did as she was commanded.

Dovid was shuddering so hard it felt as if he might come out of his skin as he watched his mother try to cover her nakedness with her hands.

The guards paid no heed. They forced the Levis forward with eight other Jews until they came to a massive, deep wide canyon. Then the Jews were lined up at the edge of the gorge.

Dovid felt his heart leap into his throat. His body was paralyzed with fear. He couldn't move. He had to move, he had to help them, but he couldn't. Tears rushed down his cheeks as he realized his helplessness.

His mother was weeping. His father took her into his arms. A soldier yelled, "Let go of her and stand straight." His father ignored the command. It didn't matter anymore. Dovid knew it. He knew what was coming. OH GOD! And he could see that his parents knew it too. They were to be shot, murdered, and thrown into the ravine. This was the future that the Nazis had planned for the Jews of Kiev. Dovid's papa had been right not to trust them.

Dovid felt the breath leave his body as the soldier pulled his gun.

NO, please God NO! God, please do something to stop them, Dovid screamed inside of his head as he watched the bullets enter his parents' bodies. The sound was deafening. It was a sound that would wake him in nightmares for the rest of his life. Dovid's Mama and Papa fell like ragdolls into the deep pit but the young girl who had been standing beside his mother was still alive, even after she'd been shot. She dropped to the ground holding her stomach as she bled out onto the earth. One of the soldiers saw her and laughed. He turned to his fellow Nazis and said something in German. Then they all laughed. The girl lay there on the ground bleeding. She couldn't be more than sixteen.

The soldier walked over to her and shot her again, this time in the head. Blood and brain matter splattered the man's boots and uniform. Dovid puked up bile from his empty stomach. Now the young girl lay still. Her face was gone. In its place was a mass of bloody matter. With his black boot, the Nazi kicked the girl's body into the gorge.

Dovid had seen enough. Silent as a cat, he ran out the back of the cemetery and away from the horror he'd just witnessed. He ran, and he ran. He kept running until the stitch in his side hurt so badly that he had to stop and sit down for a few minutes. Never before had Dovid felt such hatred toward anyone.

Dovid sat under a tree for a few minutes. Visions of what he had just seen haunted him. He got up and began to run again. He ran, and he ran, his feet flying beneath him, as he put time and distance between himself and the Nazis. Finally, after forty-five minutes of racing at top speed, Dovid Levi fell to his knees and wept. Although he'd seen his parents' murder with his own eyes it was hard to believe that it had really happened.

Today I became an orphan.

CHAPTER TWELVE

✡

A boy can only lie in the dirt crying for so long. Then he must rise and go forward to find his destiny, to live in the future. And so it was with Dovid. His face stained black from earth mixed with tears, he began to head back to the farmhouse. As he walked, he watched his feet, step after step. He could not raise his head to face the sunshine.

How could I stand there and watch those bastards kill my parents and do nothing? I am a coward. A coward.

Then something akin to a bright light flickered inside of Dovid and he realized that he was not going to return to the Ivanov's farm. No, he had a more important job to do than farming. Today, he was going to enlist as Oskar Ivanov, in the Red Army. No one need know that he was a Jew. He hated the Soviets. He'd heard his parents talk about how Stalin was a terrible dictator who hated Jews. But even though he had no love for Stalin, he would use the Soviets to fight the Nazis because Dovid hated the Nazis more. Over the last several hours Dovid had gone from being a sheltered and protected child to an angry and bitter man with a debt to pay.

Whether I live or die is not important. I will make those Nazis sorry for the death of my parents. From this day forward, I vow to do whatever I can to rid the world of the filthy Third Reich.

CHAPTER THIRTEEN

✡

Having grown up learning a great deal about the medical profession from his father, Dovid also knew a lot about how things were done concerning the registering of births. He was fairly sure that because Oskar Ivanov was born on a farm, he would have been delivered by midwives and his exact birth date probably never registered. Therefore, when Dovid enlisted in the army under the name of Oskar Ivanov, he easily lied about his age. At the recruiting office they asked him several questions. Dovid convinced them that he was seventeen. But more importantly, that he was a staunch supporter of the Soviet Union, communism, and that he longed to serve his homeland and his leader, Joseph Stalin. Dovid made known his hatred for the Germans and his desire to push them back to their own land and off Soviet soil. The recruiters were impressed by this young man with the dark deep mysterious eyes and the strong convictions. And before he knew it, Dovid, now Oskar Ivanov, was a soldier in the armed forces of the USSR.

CHAPTER FOURTEEN

✡

Hand-to-hand combat will reveal a man's true nature. It is there that he is sure to discover if he is a hero, or a sadist, or someone in between. His inner strength to conquer his own fears will be tested. He will stare at the stars at night and wonder what happens after death. He will question what is good and what is evil. But most of all, as he is witness to so much death, he will ponder the meaning of life itself. For some men, being close to death and violence will drive them mad. Others will find the inner strength to keep a firm grasp on their sanity even as they watch their friends fall all around them. And finally, war will test a man's fortitude. As this same man looks into the eyes of someone he has never met before, but calls his enemy because of the uniform he wears, will he be able to pull the trigger and end that man's life? Yes, war, and in particular. hand-to-hand combat, will strip a person naked and lay him bare before his own eyes.

Battle was already raging in Moscow between the Nazi invaders and the Red Army when Oskar Ivanov arrived. The winter of 1941 had started early and had proven to be one the coldest that Oskar could remember. The tires on the cars and tanks froze. Oskar's fingers and nose were numb and he was constantly afraid of frostbite. Even though he had socks and heavy boots, his toes ached. The temperature hovered around ten below zero. Upon his arrival in the city, Oskar was immediately taken to his platoon. On the way he saw that deep ditches surrounded the city.

"Who dug those? The soldiers?" Oskar asked one of his comrades. Oskar was wondering if he was going to be digging ditches in the freezing air.

"No. It was the citizens of Moscow. They have been helping us. They don't want the German tanks coming into their city any more than we do."

But the ditches couldn't stop the Germans.

And the horrors of war and bloodshed quickly became part of Oskar's daily routine.

Oskar had been full of anger and bravado when he enlisted. But now, as he scanned the burning city, he saw the pools of blood against the white snow, the scattered dead bodies of Germans and Russians with missing limbs, severed heads, and gouged-out eyes. He realized the only thing distinguishing Russian bodies from German bodies were the uniforms. It wasn't the young boys who were lying dead in the snow who'd asked for this calamity. It was the leaders of their countries. In particular, it was one terrible man…Adolf Hitler. There was a smell to war. It was an odor of fear, mixed with gunpowder and smoke. As he settled into his makeshift barracks, Oscar's fingers tapped the cool metal of the gun that he wore at his side.

Anyone who observed him would have thought him a tough and fearless fighter, but Dovid Levi, the thirteen-year-old Jewish boy who hid inside of Oskar, was afraid. Although Oskar was a member of a battalion, he had never felt so alone before in his entire life. He had also never felt so young. It was as if he realized for the first time that he was only a boy, and must somehow find the inner strength to be ready to accept death should it be his fate.

The first time he killed a man, Oskar vomited. He shot his gun and saw blood shoot out of the man's eye. Then he saw the man fall. Without warning, the contents of Oskar's stomach emptied onto the snow. His fellow soldiers laughed at him.

"You'll get used to it," one of them said.

It was not the sight of blood that had sickened him to the point of puking. He'd worked with his father in medicine. Blood, broken limbs, and injuries were commonplace in a doctor's office. What had reached inside of Oskar/Dovid and squeezed his gut until he expelled everything inside of him was the fact that he, Dovid Levi, had caused the loss of a life. He had taken a life away from another human being. Yes, he hated the Nazis and yes, he'd vowed to kill them if he could. But in his heart, Dovid was not a murderer. He respected God's gift of life. His father had reared him to be a healer, not a killer. The young soldier, with blood oozing from the space where his eye had been, was no more than a boy. It was not as if this boy had murdered his parents. Dovid Levi could not justify having taken a life in his own mind. Life and death were God's business. He had his bar mitzvah only a few months ago. He knew God's commandments. And he also knew that he'd broken one.

At that point, Dovid would have liked to have left the army and gone back to the farm. But there was no leaving. Stalin did not allow his men to retreat. No, Dovid must not look back. There was no way back. He was Oskar Ivanov now. He was a soldier in the Red Army and he must continue to kill Nazis. This was his fate, this was the song that he had heard the flute player playing and he must dance to it, even though everything about committing murder felt wrong.

As the weeks passed and he saw his friends

die, the killing of the enemy did become surprisingly easier. However, Oskar found that he could be more useful to his comrades by practicing the medical training that he'd learned as a boy. He bandaged wounds, removed bullets, and stitched up gashes. This he found rewarding. This he could do with good conscience. And so he did. During battle, Oskar became fearless because his mind was not on the killing, it was on the healing. He was usually the first man to run out into the field to help a dying Soviet soldier.

CHAPTER FIFTEEN

✡

December 7, 1941.

The Japanese bombed Pearl Harbor and the Americans entered the war. The Japanese were linked with the Germans. Hitler was already engaging in an all-out battle to take Britain. The Americans allied with the British.

In June of 1942, Hitler set his sights on Stalingrad. At first it appeared that the Germans would take the city. The Nazis moved forward and by October of 1942 they reached the shores of the Volga.

However, two important events occurred that changed the outlook for Hitler. In August of the same year, Winston Churchill and the United States came to the aid of the Soviet Union. The British and the Americans began to send ammunition and manpower in order to help Stalin defeat the Nazis. And the second crucial event was that the Nazis had counted on taking Stalingrad before the deadly cold Russian winter descended upon them.

The USSR was a sea of vast and open land, making it difficult for Hitler to get supplies to his troops once the winter set in. Hitler tried to send what he could by plane. But the truth was that the Nazi soldiers were starving and, because they had insufficient clothing, they were freezing to death. With the help of the Americans and the British, the cards were stacked against Hitler's Third Reich.

CHAPTER SIXTEEN

✡

If Oskar had been horrified at the battle in Moscow he was aghast in Stalingrad. Never had he seen such carnage on both sides.

However, it was in the heat and danger of this battle that Oskar learned that he, little Dovid Levi, had the courage of the lion of Judea. However, it wasn't through murder or shooting a thousand Nazis that he found his heroism. It was through love and through healing. For the first time, he could feel what it meant to be the son of a great doctor. For he knew now that although his father had left the earth, his papa would never really die because he, Dovid Levi, carried his father's genes in his blood.

Oskar had been hiding alone in a foxhole trying to stay silent, even though he could not help coughing from the smoke all around him. He peeked over the edge to see where the enemy was and just as he did he saw a superior officer take a bullet several feet in front of him. There were dead and dying men all around him. Blood soaked the ground. Oskar was afraid that the same fate awaited him. He wanted to burrow into the ground like a mole, and he could have stayed in the foxhole and protected himself if he had chosen to. No one would have been the wiser. There was far too much confusion for anyone to know where he was. But, even against the thunder of the guns blasting, Oskar imagined he could hear the wheezing breath of the man whom he had just seen shot. Again, Oskar stole a glance out of the trench. He could see that the life was pouring out of the officer's body, spilling crimson onto the snow. Without assistance this man would surely die. Oskar curled back into the earth and tried to ignore the sound.

Am I really hearing him? This doesn't make sense. How can I hear that man dying when the noise of gunfire and bombings all around me is deafening?

Then Oskar shivered because he thought he

heard his father's voice.

"Dovid, you have to help that man. You will be all right. Go now. Put your faith in me and leave the foxhole. Bring that officer back here to the trench with you. Move quickly. I will watch over you. You will be safe, my son. You will not take a bullet."

I am going mad. I must be going mad. I am hearing the voice of my dead father. I can't leave this place. If I stand up I will be an open target, Oskar thought. He was puzzled because his father's words were as clear as if his father were sitting right by his side. Then, once again, Oskar heard his father say, "Go Dovid. Go now; get the man. Hurry, run." Driven by his father's prompting, Oskar put his trust in God and left the safety of the foxhole. He got to his feet and, still hunched over, ran to the officer's side. As he did, he heard a bullet whisk by his face, missing him by inches, but he didn't flinch. Grabbing the man's arm, Oskar dragged the officer back to the trench. Two more gunshots missed Oskar by inches. He heard them but he did not fear. It was as if a white light surrounded him. Somehow he knew he would survive. Once he and the officer were back in the foxhole, Oskar examined the man. The officer had been shot in the leg and was losing a lot of blood. Oskar took off his belt and tightened it around the man's leg to stop the bleeding. Then as soon as he was able, Oskar dragged the officer to the medic's tent where he took care of the officer's wound.

CHAPTER SEVENTEEN

✡

Although Oskar didn't know it at the time, he'd saved the life of an important man that day. That man vowed never to forget the boy who had risked his own safety in order to rescue him. With a little influence, from that day forward, Oskar began to work full time as a medic instead of being on the front lines of battle. He put his healing talent that his father had passed on to him to good use, proving himself a hero again and again. And so it was that Oskar gained the respect and friendship of his superiors.

Although Oskar never voiced his opinions to anyone, he felt that the Soviet army was brutal to its soldiers. He hated to see any form of cruelty and injustice. A deserter could easily be sent to a concentration camp in Siberia. But not only that, Oskar never forgot that his parents always hated Stalin because Stalin hated the Jews. His father had said that

Stalin was not a friend of the Jewish people. Perhaps it began with Stalin's jealousy of Trotsky? Oskar couldn't remember everything his parents had said. The truth was that at the time he hadn't been listening. It wasn't important to him. After all, he'd been just an innocent boy then. But now he wanted to know more about the government for which he was fighting. He wished more than anything that he could talk to his father even just one more time. He didn't understand so many things. So many things he would have liked for his father to explain. And besides wanting to ask his parents questions, he often thought he would give anything to be with his parents, even for just a few minutes. To hear their voices, to touch their skin, to feel the comfort of his mother's hand on his forehead. But it was too late. They were dead. He saw them both die a horrible death. And at fourteen years old, Oskar was a soldier and he was totally and completely on his own in the world.

CHAPTER EIGHTEEN

✡

December 1942
Stalingrad.

The Russians fired a barrage of missiles at the Germans, who were now completely out of ammunition. The Nazis were like walking skeletons, shivering in the below zero temperatures. Georgy Zhukov, the Soviet General in charge, strategically placed his troops to surround the German army. The Nazis were like mice in the grip of a gang of powerful felines. Friedrich Paulus, the general in charge of the German troops, had no choice. He was forced to retreat. Hitler had made a fatal mistake. He'd underestimated his Soviet neighbors. And so, in February 1943, General Paulus was forced to surrender.

Joseph Stalin was delighted that the Soviet army had never lost control of Stalingrad. After all, it was the city that bore his name.

CHAPTER NINETEEN

✡

Late summer, 1944

Dovid's platoon waited in the outskirts of Warsaw while the Home Army struggled to fight the Nazis in the streets of the city. Stalin had sent direct orders to his troops to do nothing to help the Polish. Instead, the Soviet leader was laying in wait for Poland to be defeated and weak. Once the Polish resistors had lost the battle, the Russian troops marched into the city. They took Warsaw from the Germans but instead of freeing Poland, the country was now under Soviet rule.

The Red Army marched forth through their newly conquered land. As they tore through war-ravaged Poland, they began to witness the evidence of the crimes that the Nazis had left behind. The most eye-opening spectacle of true horror began when they started liberating the concentration camps. Any Nazis that they found, they executed. But most had already tucked their tails between their legs and fled like cowards.

Oskar entered the barbed-wire walls of the concentration camp with the rest of his troop. The stench was so strong that he ran behind a building where no one could see him and vomited. Although he'd been on the battlefield, he'd never seen so many piles of dead bodies as he saw at this camp. But unlike the battlefield, these were not soldiers. These were the bodies of women, children, old men, all of them naked and starved until their bones jutted out from their flesh. The horror of it made it seem almost unreal. There were also people still there on the grounds of the camp that had by some miracle survived the Nazis' attempts to kill them. They were limping or wandering slowly around the abandoned camp looking lost and unsure of where to go or what to do. Dovid was shocked at their bodies; they were as gaunt and gray as the dead. Some of the Russian soldiers, who had religious backgrounds, crossed themselves in revulsion when they saw the inhumanity that had gone on in the camps, even though the Soviet government demanded that they abandon any religious attachments. Oskar was surprised to see that a few of his fellow soldiers even had tears in their eyes.

When the Soviets entered the camps, the prisoners fell to their knees and kissed the boots of their liberators.

"Who are you? What happened here?" one of the soldiers asked. "Are you political prisoners?"

"Some of us are. But mostly we are Jews, gypsies, homosexuals, Jehovah's Witnesses.'"

"What were you arrested for?"

"I was arrested for being a Jew."

The soldier didn't say another word. But it didn't matter. Oskar had heard enough to send him back in his mind to the day that his parents died. He had a vision. He was suddenly standing alone behind a tree, watching the monstrous murder of thousands of innocent people taking place at Babi Yar.

And he was once again Dovid. Dovid Levi, a thirteen-year-old innocent Jewish boy, the son of a doctor. People were moving around on all sides of him but Dovid was lost in his memory. He could see the children holding their mothers' hands as they waited in line to be shot and thrown into that terrible mass grave. Dovid's palms began to sweat. He felt dizzy and nauseated. He put both hands over his eyes to somehow blot out the vision. But he couldn't get it out of his head. So he leaned against the gray building next to a pile of dead bodies and began to hyperventilate.

"Ivanov. Get a hold of yourself." Oskar's superior officer shook Oskar hard. "Get a hold of yourself, I tell you."

Dovid remembered that he was not Dovid anymore. He was Oskar Ivanov, a soldier in the Soviet army. He nodded, trying hard to draw breath. "I need a minute. I'm sorry."

"Well hurry it up. There is no time for you to stand here and act like a woman. We have to move forward. We are soldiers, Ivanov. We have work to do."

Yes. Work to do. Oskar thought, and he forced himself to put the visions from the past out of his mind.

Oskar's platoon went on to liberate two more camps. The atrocities that Oskar saw were reminders to him of who he was and what it meant to be a Jew. At one of the camps he met a man who was close to his own age. There was an immediate connection between them.

"I'm Moishe Finkelstein," the former concentration camp prisoner introduced himself. Oskar nodded, feeling that somehow this man knew he was a Jew.

"You're free now," Oskar said, not knowing what else to say.

"Free? I have no home, no family, no place to go. I am free. I am alive. But everyone I love and everything I know is gone. I saw my family killed. I have no one to look for. What is left for me?"

"I'm sorry," Oskar said. "I don't know what to tell you to do…"

"I know what I must do. Now it's just a matter of finding a way to do it. Remember this Oskar, if a man can get out of Europe he should. Especially if he is a Jew, Oskar. The place to be is the United States of America. That's my goal. To get to America. There everyone is treated equally. There, I will be able to live freely as a Jew."

Oskar nodded, wanting to run away from this haunting man with his death mask face and emaciated body. He longed to be free of Moishe's words of wisdom.

"You know, my name is Moishe. You know what that means right?"

"Moses."

"Yes, the deliverer. You are a Jew, Oskar. I know it. I can tell. It's all right, you need not say a word. But, heed my advice. Get out of Europe, Oskar. Get out as soon as you can."

"Here." Oskar handed Moishe the food he had in his pack "Eat this and good luck to you," Oskar said and turned to leave.

"Remember. If you can find a way to get out

of Europe, go to America. Russia is no good either. They are unkind to Jews, too," Moishe said.

"What makes you think I am a Jew?"

"I know it," Moishe said.

"You are wrong," Oskar answered curtly.

"Am I?" Moishe smiled and the bones in his cheeks became even more pronounced. "Thank you for the bread," Moishe said as Oskar walked away quickly.

Oskar was glad to move on with his platoon. But the eyes of Moishe, the Jew, were burned in his mind.

What was it about that man's message that cut to the core of me? And how in the hell did he know that I am a Jew?

That night, Oskar had a dream of his parents. They were sitting at the Sabbath table on a Friday night. He could hear the prayers. When he awakened to his superior officer's voice his face was wet with tears.

"Let's go, let's get moving," his superior

officer yelled to the entire troop. "There is no time to lose. We must beat the Americans to Berlin so we can get a hold on the city before they do."

So Oskar's battalion moved ever forward towards Berlin, the heart of Hitler's Reich. Marching tirelessly to be the first of the Allies to arrive there.

And then…the Red Army entered Germany.

CHAPTER TWENTY

✡

Oskar and his fellow soldiers hated the Germans. After all, they'd been in battle with the Nazis, who had killed their friends and wounded their brothers. Now they entered the country of their enemy as conquerors and most of them were heady with power. All of the German men of fighting age were gone, leaving the vulnerable women and children behind. To add more fuel to the fire, the soldiers had been at war and had not been with women for a long time. The German women were alone and hated by the Soviets, who were more than happy to take revenge by raping them and stealing what little they had left. The soldiers were young men who were starved for sex and they had the power to take what they wanted. After all, there was no one to stop them.

CHAPTER TWENTY-ONE

✡

On the eve of Hitler's suicide, the Red Army entered Berlin. They tore down the flag with the swastika and raised the Soviet flag. Victory was sweet. They forced two women to take them into their homes. The house where Oskar was staying was owned by an old German woman. It was a nice-sized home with several bedrooms and a sofa in the living room. Oskar felt a little odd sleeping on a bed when the old woman was forced to sleep on the floor. But he would not go against his comrades and give up his bed. He would do just as they did, even though everything in his upbringing told him it was wrong.

Once the soldiers were settled in their new home they went out to get drunk. Oskar and his fellow soldiers went into pubs where they refused to pay but drank to their victory until they could drink no more. When they were so intoxicated they were unable to walk straight, they decided to head back to the old lady's house where they could get some rest. On their way, they saw a young slender woman. She was walking quickly with her head down. Oskar could not see her face. Until now, Oskar had not been present during any of the gang rapes that the other soldiers committed but from the look of mischief in his fellow soldiers' eyes, Oskar knew that they intended to do harm to the girl. He dared not try to stop them. Instead, he turned away, trying to ignore what he could not ignore. One of the men chased the girl. He caught her and grabbed her then he pushed her into an alleyway between two buildings.

"No, please," she said in German. Oskar had little trouble understanding. She looked up and Oskar looked away. Two of the soldiers threw her on the ground. Oskar stayed a good distance away, but even from where he stood it was easy to see that they were taking turns with her. She was crying, screaming and pleading with them to stop and let her be. Oskar felt the bile rise in his throat. The voice of his father tried to come into his head, but he refused to allow it in.

"Come on, Oskar. It's your turn," one of the soldiers said.

"I don't feel like it," Oskar said, leaning against the building.

"Come on…you're not a fagot are you? Don't tell me you're a fagot after I have been sleeping next to you for months," another of the soldiers said.

"You know I haven't seen Oskar fuck any of the women we have been fucking. He always seems to be absent. Perhaps you are a pervert. Maybe it's boys you like? You like cock, Oskar?" one of the other soldiers said, mocking him dangerously.

They were taunting him. No one knew it but Oskar was still a virgin. He'd never had sex. He'd often had the desire for a woman but the ideal situation had never arisen. However, a woman begging for her life on the pavement in an alley was not the way he had envisioned his first time.

"Leave me alone," Oskar said.

"So, you do like cock? You go for men."

"Leave me alone. I don't need to force a girl. If a woman doesn't want me where is the fun in it?" Oskar said, trying to sound casual. But he felt sick and scared. If they thought he was a homosexual they would make his life a living hell. He knew how cruel these men who were now his temporary friends could be.

"After so many months without a good fuck, if you're not queer you'd be grabbing at this."

"So, Oskar, are you queer or are you going to do it?"

Oskar looked into the faces of his fellow soldiers. He knew if he didn't have intercourse with this girl that things would change for him as far as his fellow soldiers were concerned. These men would lose respect for him. They would doubt his sexuality and he'd be punished severely for being what they detested, a homosexual. Trying to appear nonchalant, Oskar unzipped his pants. He stood over the girl. She was still crying. Oskar tried not to look at her face, especially her eyes. If he looked into her eyes and felt pity for her he would never be able to go through with this. Her dress was pulled up over her waist and her panties were torn. He'd never seen a woman's parts before. And as much as he was repulsed by the idea of a gang rape, his body responded to her nakedness. He hid his naked penis with his hand lest anyone saw that he was circumcised and suspected that he was a Jew. To his shame, his penis became erect and against his own will, he entered her. It was over in minutes. His body trembled in orgasm, but his heart was filled with disgrace. Oskar stood up and closed his pants.

Three more men had their way with the poor girl. She'd stopped crying now. In fact, she was terrifyingly silent. Oskar watched them, feeling a strong sense of self-loathing. How could he have felt so much pleasure in the animal act itself, all the while knowing that he was inflicting so much pain on another person? Where is Dovid Levi? Son of

Menachem and Raisa Levi?

Papa, Mama, I am so ashamed.

Once the soldiers were done with the girl they began to walk back towards the house where they were staying.

"I'll be right back," Oskar said.

"Where are you going?" one of his comrades asked.

"It seems that my wallet fell out of my pocket in the alley."

"Do you remember how to get back to the house where we are staying or should I come with you?"

"Yes, I remember. You go on ahead. I'll be there soon." Oskar said.

"Good. We'll meet you there."

Oskar nodded. He turned the corner and as he did, he saw the girl. She was walking quickly, hugging herself. Even from where he stood he could see a trickle of blood running down her leg. He ran towards her. She cowered in fear and bent at the waist to protect herself when she saw him.

"I came to tell you that I am sorry. I know it can't mean much to you. But I am sorry," he said.

She nodded. He could see that her hand that was around her waist was trembling. She was afraid of him. He hated to see that he, Dovid Levi, had struck fear in another human being.

"Here," he said, taking his day's ration of bread out of his backpack. "Here, take this please," he said, feeling like he wanted to cry.

She shook her head and pulled into herself.

"Please, take it. I beg you to take it."

She looked up at him. This was the first time that he noticed her eyes were blue. Before this moment, he hadn't really seen her. She wasn't exceptionally beautiful. In fact, she was plain. Her plainness made him feel worse. *She is just a young girl alone and frightened. How could I do that? What is wrong with me?*

The girl would not take the food. She just stood there looking at him like a frightened deer. "Please let me go home," she said.

"What's your name?" He'd asked her name so he could make her feel less victimized. But it had the opposite effect. She didn't want to tell him.

"Please…" she said. "Please let me go. My name is Christine."

"Christine. My name is Oskar. I know you are afraid of me. And you have every right to be. But please, know that I am sorry." Then in a choked up voice he said, "God knows I am sorry. But I want to do something nice for you. So I am going to leave this food here on the ground. I know you won't take it directly from me. But it is right over here and it would be good for you to take it home to your family. I will not bother you anymore. I am leaving now. I am so very sorry, Christine. My parents didn't raise me to treat women like this," he said, then he turned and left. Turning the corner, he never looked back to see if she'd taken the food. But he hoped she had.

Oskar would always remember that day as the first time he saw how a man's own body could betray him. And how even he, Oskar, was capable of doing things he despised.

From then on, to avoid being pressured or harassed, Oskar made a point of finding and being seen with women of questionable repute. They wore tight skirts and low cut blouses. And because he was growing into a handsome man and wore a Soviet uniform, he found he had no lack of women eager to share his bed and receive the little extras he as a soldier was able to give them. As time passed, his fellow soldiers began to give him nicknames like "Romeo."

Three years later, Oskar was transferred to Warsaw where he was promoted to a good position working in the local police station. There in Poland, Oskar still had a constant flow of nameless women who came into his life in the evening and left in the morning. Many nights he drank too much vodka in an attempt to drown out his memories of his parents and all that he'd grown up to believe was right and wrong. It made it easier to embrace his supremacy as a member of the Soviet aristocracy. He was enjoying the better life that was bestowed upon Stalin's favorites. And, sometimes, he was even able to bury the young Dovid Levi whom he'd once been.

Then in the fall of 1948, a group of Yiddish writers was arrested by the Soviet government. Dovid heard about it because it was considered big news. The following summer, several more Yiddish writers were arrested. They were all known to be members of the Jewish Anti-Fascist Committee. Everyone was discussing the arrests, and Oskar could not help but overhear his co-workers talking about the Jewish traitors. Jewish! The word Jewish! It was so easy for them to hate these people because they were Jewish. Dovid wondered if the writers were really responsible for all that they were accused of or if they were being attacked simply because they were Jews. It was dangerous to talk openly about government policies unless one was in complete agreement. However, Dovid heard through whispers of those who did not agree that the Jewish writers were being tortured for espionage and treason.

"They are beating them badly. I believe that it is because they are Jews. But don't quote me," one of Oskar's good friends spoke very softly to him over lunch one day.

"You think so?" Oskar asked, hoping it was not true, although a part of him feared that it was. He had, after all, fought for the Soviet regime.

"Of course. Stalin hates Jews. After all, who doesn't? They are untrustworthy and get what they deserve. Don't you agree?"

"Yes, of course." Oskar nodded. But this conversation felt like a boulder in his belly. It hurt his heart. too. A distant memory of Dovid Levi helping the poor and the sick crept back into his mind. Oskar tried to convince himself that he'd put his Jewish roots behind him. But he had only covered them, buried them with dirt. But now, they were like tiny delicate blades of grass coming up, rising up.

I have been posing as a Soviet but I was born a Jew. My wonderful parents were Jews and were they still alive they would be ashamed of how I have been living. But if my Soviet friends ever learned that I am Jewish they would forget the bonds of our friendship and I would be nothing but a Jew to them.

Oskar also realized something else. Something that came to him while he was walking to work one day. *All of my running around with different women is because I don't want to marry someone who is not Jewish.* He secretly longed to celebrate Shabbat with his wife and children. He wanted his parents to see him from wherever they were as he took his bershart, the woman God had ordained for him, under a chuppah, a canopy, and said his marriage vows. That was why Oskar was unable to settle down. It was as if he'd had a revelation that day. And now he understood himself better.

CHAPTER TWENTY-TWO

✡

In 1953, Joseph Stalin died of a brain aneurysm. But the iron fist that held the people clasped under Soviet rule did not die with him. His successor, Nikita Khrushchev, would carry on where Stalin left off.

CHAPTER TWENTY-THREE

✡

Warsaw, Spring 1956

Ela Dobinski looked into her mother's eyes with genuine concern. She had truly believed that her Mama would be happy to hear that she'd chosen to join the convent. After all, Helen had raised her to love the Catholic religion. Ela couldn't understand why her mother was acting so strangely.

"The story I am about to tell you is not an easy one for me to talk about. I have hidden the truth from you for a very long time," Helen said, choking on her words

"The truth, Mama?"

"Yes. Ela, my sweet precious daughter. When you first told me that you wanted to become a nun I felt that it was God's way of forgiving me for my sins. But then, I began to think about your decision and consider it more deeply. And, well, there are things you don't know. And these are things you must know before you decide for sure that you want to become a nun."

"Like what, Mama? Like what?" Ela was nervous. She drummed her fingers on the kitchen table.

"Let me put up a pot of water for tea and I will tell you everything. It is time," Helen said, pouring water into the kettle. When the tea was done Helen poured a cup for Ela and one for herself. She was so unraveled that she burned her hand on the stove. Ela got up and looked at her mother's fingers, which were red.

"Mama, you burned yourself." Ela kissed Helen's hand. "What is it that's wrong? I don't understand. You are acting so strangely. Please, Mama, what is it? Please, you must tell me."

"I am so afraid that once I tell you, everything that we have built as mother and daughter will change between us."

"Nothing will ever change between us. Not ever…"

Helen took a deep breath. Then she sighed. *I must begin. No matter what the consequences are, I must tell her,* Helen thought and then she began to explain. "Do you remember … it was long ago. You were just a child. It was the day that you won the jump rope contest. You were so excited. Do you remember that day?"

"Of course, I remember. I only won one time," Ela smiled. "But what does all of this have to do with anything?"

"There was a lady here in our home when you came upstairs. Do you recall? She had dark hair and there was a man here with her?"

"I do remember her, actually. She had such deep eyes. I recall that I was afraid of her."

"Yes. I know you were. And I told you that you had nothing to ever fear from her."

"Yes, you told me that later that night."

"That woman…she was Jewish. She lived through the war. Her name was Zofia Weiss. She was imprisoned in the ghetto by the

Nazis. I don't know if she was ever in a concentration camp. But she might have been."

"That is probably why her face looked so severe. But what does all of this have to do with me? With us?"

"Well… there is more. And, I don't know how to tell you this. So, I will just blurt out what I have to say. Ela, that woman was your birth mother. Your real name is Eidel Weiss. When you were very young, your mother and I arranged to have you smuggled out of the ghetto."

Ela looked at Helen with her eyes open wide. "How could this be? You've been lying to me all of this time about being my mother? This is insane! Why? Why didn't you tell me the truth?"

"Because we loved you. She and I both loved you."

"I don't understand."

"Ela, you know how people feel about the Jews. I couldn't tell you. You were just a child.

It was too dangerous. You know how children are. They speak without thinking. If you had said even the smallest thing that gave away the truth about your birth when you were young and the Nazis found out, they would have taken you away from me. And probably sent you to a camp. Or they might even have killed you."

"And when I got older? After the Soviet takeover? Why didn't you tell me then?"

"Do you think that the Soviets like Jews? You should know better. You hear plenty of people complain about the Jewish people. They are always under scrutiny. It was just easier if you didn't know. Better for you. At least that is what I believed. Then."

Ela got up and walked away from Helen. She looked out the window down at the courtyard where she had been jumping rope that day when she'd seen the woman, Zofia Weiss, whom she had just learned was her birth mother.

"Ela, this is for you. It was your mother's." Helen took the gold Star of David necklace out of the pocket of her housecoat and handed it to Ela.

"This was my mother's?"

Helen nodded. Ela held up the chain and looked at the charm. "This is the same symbol that the Jews wore sewn on their clothes during the war. Isn't it?"

Again, Helen nodded.

"What was she like?"

"Zofia? She was my very good friend. That was why I agreed to take you. We both wanted to save your life. It was dangerous for me and Papa too."

"Where is she now?"

"I don't know."

Ela held the necklace in her fist. "I want to go to my room, Mama. I need some time alone."

"I understand. But I couldn't let you join the convent without knowing the truth," Helen said.

Ela nodded but did not turn and look at

Helen. Instead, she went into her room and closed the door.

CHAPTER TWENTY-FOUR

✡

Ela didn't come out in the morning, and Helen decided not to bother her. She was terrified that the close relationship that she shared with her daughter would end because of the lies. But she'd done what she had to do. Now it was only a matter of waiting to see what the consequences would be for her choices.

Ela didn't go to school that day, but Helen went to work. When she got home, Ela had prepared dinner and was sitting at the kitchen table.

Helen put her handbag down on the lumpy sofa and took off her hat and her jacket.

"Mama," Ela said. "Whether I am Ela Dobinski or Eidel Weiss, I love you. You are my mother. You are the woman who raised me, who cared for me when I was sick, who held me when I cried. I have to admit, I would like to find this Zofia Weiss. I would like to talk to her, to know more about her and my background. But, no matter what happens, you are and will always be my mother. After all, she gave me up. You took me in."

"No, Ela. She never gave you up. It wasn't like that at all. If she could have kept you she would have. It hurt her terribly to let you go. She saved your life. Together, she and I saved your life. Zofia Weiss loved you. Never forget that. She made the ultimate sacrifice for you. She gave you up so you might live."

"It's all so emotionally confusing, Mama. But I am glad you told me. And, considering what I now know, I don't think I will join the convent."

"Be careful, Ela. Don't tell anyone about your background. If people know that your mother was Jewish, they will treat you differently. And if the government finds out they will stamp your papers. You know that I don't have any bad feelings towards Jews. But so much of the rest of the world seems to be against them. Why do that to yourself if you don't have to?"

Ela nodded. "You're right. Mama. But it seems so unfair. That poor woman. What was the ghetto like? What does it mean to be a Jew? I don't even know…"

"The ghetto was a terrible place. You've seen where it stood."

"Yes, but I never thought much about it until now."

"When you were just a little girl, the Nazis rounded up all the Jewish people and sent them to the ghetto where they kept them like prisoners. They were very mean to them. Terrible. You ask me what it means to be a Jew. I don't know because I am not one. But I saw how the Jewish people suffered in that ghetto, Ela. They were starving and sick. Many people living in one room. No food. No heat. Lots of disease. The Nazis were very cruel to the Polish, but they were even worse to the Jews."

"How did you two get me out?"

"Your mother had a good friend, an old lady

whom she had apprenticed under as a seamstress. The old lady made a deal with some fellow who was working in the underground and he smuggled you out."

"The underground?"

"Yes, he was leaving the ghetto at night to buy weapons and food, which he brought back inside the ghetto walls the following day."

"Weapons? Did the Jews fight back?"

"Yes. They tried; there was an uprising. They fought very bravely. But there were too many Nazis who were too heavily armed and they lost."

"Was I still there when they fought?"

"No, this man from the underground had already gotten you out one night and brought you here to me."

"You knew I was coming?"

"Yes. Zofia sent someone to find me and ask me if I would take you. I was afraid, and Papa was too. But I agreed. I wanted to care for you for Zofia. And when you first came, I thought of you as my friend's child. A beautiful little girl who I was watching for Zofia. But as time passed, I came to love you and feel like you were my own blood…"

"I guess that was why it always seemed like Papa preferred Lars. I used to be hurt by that."

"It was hard for him, Ela."

"Did Lars know anything about this?"

"No, Lars was too little."

"That's right. Of course, he was too little. I am just so puzzled. I feel like my world has been turned upside down."

Helen put her arm around Ela. She kissed her daughter's hair.

"That day so long ago when Zofia came here to our house. She came because she was finally free. She had plans to take you away with her that day."

Ela looked up into Helen's eyes. "How did you feel about letting me go? I would have been traumatized if she had taken me."

"I was terrified that she would take you. I prayed to God to help me. But she and I both loved you too much to hurt you. I can remember it as if it were yesterday. Zofia and I stood together and looked out this very window. You were downstairs jumping rope. She watched you for several minutes. And when she saw how happy and adjusted you had become to your life here as a Polish girl, she decided that it was in your best interest for you to stay with me and live as a non-Jew. It was hard for her to walk out that door, but she did it for you. So you need to remember that it is safer for you if no one knows that you have Jewish blood."

"Were you ever afraid that she'd change her mind and come back?"

"Never. She told me she would not be back. I believed her. When she left, I knew that she left because your happiness was more important to her than her own."

"Tell me a little about Zofia Weiss."

"When I knew her, she was pregnant with you. She was a seamstress. In fact, she made my wedding gown. You know the quilt on my bed, the one I have had since you were a child?"

"Yes."

"Zofia made that. She gave it to me as a wedding present."

"Was she kind? When she was young, before the war, was she pretty? Do I look like her?"

"She was very kind and very beautiful. Before the Nazis came into Poland she and I had a lot of fun. We were very close in age. And we laughed and talked…."

"I remember she had dark hair with gray streaks."

"Yes. When she was young she had very lovely long dark curls."

"She didn't look like me?"

"No. In fact, you look more like me," Helen said smiling.

"My father? I must have looked like my father. Who was my father?"

Helen looked away.

"Please, who was he? He wasn't a Nazi, was he?"

"No, he wasn't a Nazi. And yes, according to Zofia, you look a lot like him. At least that is what I gather from when she described him to me. He had the blond hair, like yours. Zofia said he was very handsome. He was her music teacher at school. She was very young and she fell in love with him. One thing led to another and she got pregnant."

"Why didn't he marry her?"

"I don't know. He disappeared. That's all she said. I am sorry."

"Disappeared?"

"He was much older than Zofia and he was an American."

"An American?" Really? Was he Jewish?"

"No, I don't think so."

"Do you know his name?"

"Donald Taylor."

151

"This is all so shocking," Ela whispered.

"I know it is. And for years I've struggled with whether to tell you or not."

"I'm glad you told me. I needed to know. Even though it is hard for me to grasp."

"I love you, Ela. You must realize that I love you as if I gave birth to you."

"I believe you. I love you too, Mama."

CHAPTER TWENTY-FIVE

✡

The news about her birth mother left Ela confused. She'd been sure that she was destined to join the convent, and now she was no longer comfortable with her decision. But she knew that she had to find work and help her mother support them. If she chose, she could have gotten a job at a factory. But factory work could be dangerous and Helen discouraged it.

"Why don't you take some classes in typing and shorthand. I have been supporting us thus far, we will survive while you go to school. Then once you're finished you can find secretarial work," Helen said.

Ela agreed, but although she never told Helen, thoughts of Zofia Weiss weighed heavily on her heart. She loved Helen and no one could ever take Helen's place as her mother. But Ela wished she could talk to Zofia. There were so many things she would have loved to ask, so many things left unanswered. And what about Donald Taylor, the mysterious American who had planted his seed and then conveniently left Poland before the Nazis came in? Who was he? So many questions rolled around in Ela's mind. Sometimes she wondered if there was some way to find people who had been in the Warsaw ghetto. But she had promised her mother that she would not mention anything to anyone about Zofia or her Jewish roots. And so, Ela kept all of her secrets buried in her heart with a hundred thousand questions and no answers.

CHAPTER TWENTY-SIX

✡

Warsaw, Fall 1957

Ela did so well in school that when she finished she landed a job working in an office steno pool, where she worked alongside several other women. She was still taking some classes in English and Russian but she was a quick study. Since she was able to type at a fairly good pace of seventy words per minute with good accuracy, she began working during the day and attending school two nights a week. Her pay was low because she was a new employee but she would get raises as time passed. And, for now, the additional money helped to provide a few extras for her mother and herself.

One night, when Ela and Helen had finished dinner and were washing the dishes, her mother's friend Artur came to the apartment. Helen introduced Ela to Artur as an old friend of hers from before the war.

"I'll finish cleaning the kitchen, Mama. You go and talk to your friend," Ela said.

Helen went into the other room and sat down with Artur. "Can I get you something to eat?" Ela heard Helen ask him. "Or perhaps a cup of tea?"

"Oh no, thank you," Artur said.

Then there was a long silence. Ela strained to hear what was being said in the other room. Why had this man come to their home?

"Helen. I've given you time. But I haven't forgotten you."

"Oh Artur," she smiled.

"Last time I came by, I think it was too soon for you."

"Too soon? Yes, I suppose it was."

"So I am here to try again. I would like to take you to dinner. Will you have dinner with me, Helen?" Ela turned off the water so she could better hear the conversation.

"I don't know what to say, Artur. I told you before that I don't think it's a good idea,"

Helen said.

Ela thought she should stop listening and forced herself to turn on the water. But later that night, when Artur had left and Ela and Helen were alone, Ela asked her mother about the man who'd come to see her.

"You knew him before the war?"

"Yes, he was a good friend of Papa's and ... he was the person who brought me the necklace from your mother."

"He knew my mother?"

"I don't think so. He got it from a friend who asked him to give it to me so I could give it to you. Artur was in the resistance." Helen didn't want to tell Ela about her lover, Eryk, or the nightmare she suffered because of Rolf the Nazi. She'd told Ela about her mother, but she didn't feel obligated to talk about her own past. Some things were best left buried. There was just too much pain in the past that she could not bear to relive. And what good would it do Ela to know that she'd had a lover when she was a married woman or that she'd been a sex slave to a sadistic Nazi? No, Ela need never know these things.

"Oh, I see," Ela said. "Did he ask the person who gave him the necklace anything about where it came from?"

"Yes, but the man gave it to him five minutes before he was executed, so Artur couldn't find out very much. I'm sorry."

"It's all right, Mother."

"The war was a terrible time for all of us, Ela."

"I know, Mama," Ela said. "So is this man going to come by to see you again?"

"I agreed to have dinner with him. I didn't want to at first."

"Really, Mama?"

"You don't think I should?" Helen asked.

"I do think you should," Ela said. She was a little uncomfortable with another person coming into their lives. It had been the two of them alone for so long. But she also felt her mother needed someone in her life and Ela loved her mother enough to want what was best for her.

"I am nervous. I haven't been out for dinner with a man in so many years."

"It will be good for you, Mama."

Artur and Helen went out three evenings later and from then on they had dinner together once a week. Sometimes they went to a restaurant. Other times Artur came to the apartment where they ate with Ela. Afterward, the three of them played cards. At first, Ela felt a little strange, a little left out, but as time passed she found that she liked Artur. And it was nice to see Helen smiling and happy with something to look forward to.

CHAPTER TWENTY-SEVEN

✡

December 1957

Most days, Ela packed a lunch to take to work with her. Restaurants and cafés were expensive. However. on a bitter winter day in December, Ela forgot her lunch at home. It wasn't like her but she had her monthly period and she'd been up most of the night with terrible cramps. When she got ready to go to work the following morning she was chilled and out of sorts. The cold always felt even more noticeable when she was menstruating. It would have been nice to take the day off of work and lie in her warm bed. But she dared not. It was a decent job and she didn't want to lose it, so she bundled herself up in a warm coat, hat, and scarf, and walked to the train. The ground was dusted with snow. A harsh wind blew right through her heavy coat and wool skirt and sweater. She felt bloated and ugly. Ela always felt that way when it was her time of the month. But the worst part of it was that she was also always hungry during her period. And so when lunchtime came and she realized that she'd left her food on the kitchen counter at home, she was almost in tears. It was far too cold to walk to the train, go home, and get her food and then eat on the train ride back. The only thing to do was either wait until she got home later that night to eat, which her noisy stomach was adamantly opposed to, or go to a café and order a light meal. It was an indulgence she would never have made if she weren't so darn hungry.

Ela wrapped her knitted scarf tight around her throat as she walked the half block to a local café. It was crowded, but she got a table by the window. After placing a modest order she blew on her hands trying to warm them. As she was looking out the window and waiting for her food, a Russian soldier approached her.

"May I share your table?" he asked.

She felt a chill run up her spine. A Russian soldier?

"I'm sorry to be so bold but there are no open tables and well... there was a chair opposite you...and, well, I thought perhaps." He smiled.

Ela looked around the restaurant and realized that the man was right. The only possible place he could sit down and eat was across from her. "Yes, of course. Please sit down," she said.

The soldier took off his coat. Ela looked up at him. He smiled. The man was older than her. From his looks, she assumed he was somewhere close to thirty. But he was sophisticated and, she decided, wildly handsome.

Ela felt a blush run from her neck all the way up to her hairline. *I really hope he thinks my face is as red as a pomegranate because of the weather and not because I am embarrassed, shy, and have no idea what to say next,* she thought.

At nineteen, Ela had been on a couple of

clumsy dates. They were both with boys she knew from the neighborhood, a year or so older. Each time, she'd found that the conversation dragged. Neither of the fellows sparked any romantic interest in Ela. And because both dates ended with quick goodbye kisses and no plans for future meetings, Ela knew that she had not been what they were looking for either.

"Thank you for allowing me to sit down," the soldier said in perfect Polish. "It's terribly cold today."

His smile is so genuine. His teeth are so white and he has the most beautiful deep-set, mysterious dark eyes, she thought. *I wish I wasn't bloated and that I had taken the time to do my hair today. I look an awful mess. And even worse, he's a Russian. My mother made me promise to stay as far away from the soldiers as possible. And yet…*

"My name is Oskar Ivanov," the man said. "And since you have been so kind as to allow me to share your table, please allow me to buy your lunch."

"Oh, you don't have to do that…"

"But I insist. It would be my pleasure. May I be so bold as to ask your name?"

"Ela Dobinski."

CHAPTER TWENTY-EIGHT

✡

Oskar didn't think Ela looked awful. In fact, he was awestruck by her innocence and beauty. He was drawn to her like he had never been drawn to any woman before. He was captivated by soft timid brown eyes and her dark, golden curls. He thought her curls looked almost like brushed gold.

She is truly lovely, but she is so young. I must admit, she's not the type of girl I usually spend my time with. This one is sweet and naive. And since I have no intentions of ever marrying, I should leave her alone. I definitely should not ask to see her again, Oskar told himself.

Even though Ela knew she was going to be late back to work, somehow it didn't matter. She'd never been late before, but she was enjoying her conversation with this fellow so much that she was willing to put her job at risk to stay. Nothing like this had ever happened to her before. Oskar was charming and had wonderful stories to tell of the time he'd spent serving in the military. She noticed that he avoided talking about combat, death, or destruction. Instead, he focused on the funny antics of his fellow soldiers. He even told amusing stories about foolish things he did. He made her laugh with him. In fact, she laughed so hard that her stomach ached. The hour went by faster than Ela realized. When she looked at her watch, she was suddenly terrified by how late she was.

"I am sorry, but I have to hurry back to work," Ela said. "I am late already."

"Oh, I'm so sorry for detaining you," Oskar said. "Will you have any problems at work for coming back later than expected?"

"I don't know. I hope not. I have never been late before," she said, standing up and pulling on her coat.

"Here is my card," Oskar said. "If you have any problems with your supervisors just contact me and I will use some influence to help you. I will see to it that you don't lose your job."

Ela put the card in her handbag. She was reluctant to go. "Thank you for lunch," she said.

"Thank you for sharing your time with me."

Ela left the restaurant. Oskar laid down the money for the check and sat staring at the tablecloth for a moment.

It's best that I let her go without asking her out again. She is too young and she is not right for me. I like loose women with no ties, he thought. Then, quickly, against his better judgment, he put on his coat and went outside to run after the beautiful young blond who had just stolen his heart.

Ela was running, and Oskar would never have caught up with her if she hadn't slipped on a patch of ice and fallen. She was sitting on the pavement with her knee bleeding, a little stunned from the fall when Oskar caught up with her.

"Ela, are you all right?"

I am so embarrassed I could die. I wish I could crawl under the sidewalk. I must look so clumsy to him, she thought.

"Are you all right?" he asked again, his voice taking on a note of genuine concern.

"Yes," she said sheepishly. "I slipped on the ice."

"Here, let me help you up."

Oskar lifted Ela. "You hurt yourself?"

"I skinned my knee."

"Let me walk you back to your job," Oskar suggested.

"I'm fine, really."

"You don't want me to walk with you?"

"I just didn't want you to feel that you had to. I mean… I know you must be busy."

"The truth is that I left the restaurant because I wanted to catch up with you. I didn't want to say goodbye, and I was afraid that if I didn't hurry you would be gone. And I would never see you again." He stopped walking and turned her to face him. Then he went on. "You see … I don't often behave like this, but, I, well, I really had a nice time with you this afternoon and I wanted to ask you if perhaps you would consider having dinner with me some evening?"

It was freezing outside and yet Ela did not feel the cold as she got lost in Oskar's dark eyes. In fact, she felt a warm glow spread through her.

"I would like that very much," she said.

"Tonight? Tomorrow night? You say when," he smiled.

She giggled. "Tomorrow. Yes, tomorrow night."

"Is eight o'clock all right?"

"Fine."

"I suppose I will need your address?"

"Yes. Do you have a pen and paper?"

Ela wrote down her address and phone number then she gave it to Oskar. "I think I should go back to my office alone," she said. "I don't want my boss to think that I am arrogant and think I can do whatever I want because I am with a Russian soldier."

"I understand. But if anyone gives you any trouble, promise me that you will let me help you."

"I will," she said.

CHAPTER TWENTY-NINE

✡

When Ela got back to work with her knee bleeding, she used her fall as an excuse for being late. Her boss didn't give her a hard time and she was very grateful. It would have been uncomfortable to contact the handsome soldier and ask him to intercede if there had been a problem. Even though he'd insisted.

The following day, Ela arrived at her office early to make up for the time she'd missed. She doubled her work production that day, taking on more than was expected of her. *It is best to keep trouble at bay,* she thought, wanting her boss to know that she was genuinely sorry for being late.

But while she was working she was thinking about Helen. How was she ever going to tell her mother about her date? Helen, she was sure, would be upset that she was going out for dinner with a Russian soldier. And, normally, she would have canceled the date after considering the effect it would have on her mother. But not this time. This man had sparked a flame inside of her that she had never known was possible.

Oskar arrived ten minutes early, looking handsome in his wool coat and uniform. He even brought a small bouquet. This was impressive because flowers were nearly impossible to come by in the winter. But when Ela introduced Oskar to Helen, she could see that Helen was skeptical of him and perhaps unsure of his intentions towards Ela. Still, surprisingly, her mother didn't protest in any way when Ela and Oskar left to go to dinner.

Oskar picked Ela up in an automobile. It was warm and comfortable and, for Ela, who was accustomed to using public transportation, it was like heaven. Oskar took Ela to a fine dining establishment where the owner was also the host. He greeted Oskar by name then seated the couple at a quiet private table in the back where they were sure to have privacy. Ela had never been to an expensive restaurant. She was nervous and intimidated by the other women in their fine dresses. And even worse, she had no idea of what to order. Somehow, she was relieved that Oskar was able to detect her insecurity. He told her that she was the loveliest woman in the room and then he offered to order for her.

"Yes, please. You order," she said smiling.

A delicious dinner by candlelight with a handsome man made Ela feel as if she were a princess. The look in Oskar's eyes when they met hers made her feel special, like she was a great beauty, a woman that men desired and strived for. No one had ever looked at her that way. And she'd never felt that she was anything but plain, at least not until that night.

However, her carefree joy was marred by the painful secret she hid in the back of her mind. What would Oskar Ivanov think of Ela Dobinski if he knew the truth? If he knew she was really Eidel Weiss, the daughter of a Jew who had been in the Warsaw ghetto? Ela was afraid that he wouldn't look at her like she was a goddess anymore.

However, if for some outrageous reason she

believed she could trust him, she would have loved to ask for his help to find Zofia Weiss. She would never ask because she was afraid to trust anyone, but she thought that if anybody could help her find Zofia it was Oskar. But when Oskar smiled at her, she realized that she was enjoying the date far too much to allow her desire to find the truth to break the spell of their wonderful evening. The fact was that Ela had never felt that good in her entire life.

For weeks, Ela forced herself not to think about Zofia. She did everything in her power to put her past behind her. Every hour that Ela was not at work she was with Oskar. If Helen had not had Artur to keep her company, Ela would have felt terrible about neglecting her mother. But the more time Ela spent with Oskar, the more often she returned home to find Artur and Helen playing cards or sharing a piece of cake. It made her smile to think that her mother had a boyfriend, but it made her giddy with delight when she thought about herself and Oskar. At night when she was alone, she wondered what it would be like to be naked in his arms. To feel his skin against hers. Then her face would turn hot with shame. After all, there was a time when she believed she had heard the calling. She had never imagined, in her wildest dreams, that she could want a man the way she wanted Oskar. Her heart, her soul, and her body sang to him, even if the tune was still silent. After all, she had not yet declared her feelings for him. And he had not declared his for her. Yet, somehow, she knew that their souls sang together in silent harmony. She felt it when he gently kissed her goodnight. She saw it in his smile when he thought she wasn't watching.

CHAPTER THIRTY

Oskar

Oskar had vowed to himself that he would never fall in love. After what he'd been through in his life, he feared love. Love meant vulnerability. It meant caring and fearing the loss of the person who had stolen one's heart. And yet, since he'd met Ela, he couldn't control himself. His heart opened up like a rose in full bloom and out of it poured all of the love he'd been telling himself he would never feel. If he had been a millionaire he would have showered her with diamonds. If he had been a farmer, he would have given her all of the crops he'd harvested.

She made him laugh, she made him think, and she terrified him by making him feel, but most of all she made him know love. And the loose women he'd been keeping company with in the past no longer held any fascination for him. He'd been on a couple of dates with two of them since he'd met Ela only to find himself returning home feeling empty and longing to see Ela. He was in love. Oskar was in love and the girl wasn't Jewish.

What would she think if she knew the truth? If she knew that he was not Oskar Ivanov, the brave and respected Russian soldier, but that he was, in fact, Dovid Levi, the son of a Jewish physician from Kiev? Would she be repulsed by his Jewish heritage? He sometimes thought about marrying her and always in his visions she stood beside him under a canopy, as is the Jewish tradition, in front of a rabbi. This, he knew, was not possible. No Catholic girl in her right mind would marry a Jewish man in a traditional Jewish ceremony. He would lose her if he ever told her the truth about who he was. And he couldn't marry her under a false pretense. Besides that, he had to keep his identity a secret from everyone. Could he even trust this woman not to tell anybody the truth about him being Jewish if she knew?

I feel as though I could and should trust her with everything that I have, with everything that I am.

Just listen to yourself, Dovid Levi. You've built a life and an image as a soldier of the Soviet army. The Soviets trust and admire you. All of this you've built on a carefully crafted lie. And now a woman, of all things, has you dancing like a marionette. You are thinking like a fool, a fool in love.

CHAPTER THIRTY-ONE

✡

Dovid considered breaking the whole thing off with Ela. He even went so far as to plan to ask for a transfer out of Warsaw. But even as he envisioned how he would leave Warsaw and forget this girl, he knew he couldn't go through with it. He was dreaming; he could never leave Warsaw and Ela behind. No, Dovid knew that he was going to ask her to marry him.

Now, his only question to himself was would he marry her as Oskar Ivanov and continue to live a lie, or would he find the courage and trust in his future wife to tell her the truth? If she did reject him and ruin his life of lies by telling the world the truth about him then she was not the woman he believed her to be.

Does it matter if she is not the saint I wish she were? The fact is, Dovid Levi, you know you would love her anyway. You are a lovesick fool.

Although he could go on living comfortably as Oskar Ivanov, he felt that he should start his life with Ela without lies between them. He would be taking a big risk and the loss could be great, but this woman was worth it to him. Still, the risk of losing her was too great. He could cope with losing the friendship and respect of his colleagues, but he couldn't cope with losing her. So, after arguing back and forth with himself for hours, he decided that he would not tell her.

His co-workers began to notice a change in Oskar. He was distracted, happy, sad, emotional. They teased him, assuming it was a woman who had stolen his heart. But what they didn't know was which woman was having such a strong effect on their friend. When girls he dated in the past came to his office to see him, he often refused to see them.

"Make some excuse for me," he usually said when they dropped by. But lately, no one had come by. There was a girl, his friends were sure of it. But they were also sure that it was someone they'd never met. And when anyone asked Oskar if he was seeing someone special, he changed the subject without giving a direct answer.

One night after having dinner with Ela, Oskar returned home. He got ready for bed and laid his clothes out for the following day. Then he began to talk to his parents in his mind.

Mama, Papa, I know you can hear me, he thought. *I am going to propose to Ela but I cannot find the words to tell her the truth about my being Jewish. I want to tell her. I know it is the right thing to do, but I cannot find a way.*

It is wrong to marry her without telling her and yet, I am afraid. In a way, I would like to marry her and then tell her when we are old. That is a silly thought, I know. And a part of me is afraid that I will never feel comfortable enough to tell her.

I have spent my life thus far alone, and I find that I am terribly lonely. This sweet girl has brought me so much joy. I have to admit that I love her and what happened before we met is important, but not as important as our future together. If she will have me, we can be wed in a civil ceremony.

But...if she insists...to make her happy...I would even agree to a Catholic wedding. Could you ever forgive me?

I am so conflicted. Sometimes I feel that I must tell her and then other times I feel that I cannot. Who am I kidding? I know how you would feel about all of this, Papa, and I am sorry, Papa. I am sorry. I know you and Mama always dreamed of my wedding. You wanted me to marry a Jewish girl under a canopy. But so much has happened since I was a boy of thirteen and you told me all of your dreams for my future on the night of my barmitzvah.

There have been so many changes in the world since then. First the Nazis then the Communists. Right now I live as a Communist. To the outside world it would seem that I embrace the Communist way of life. Which means I don't believe in God or religion. This has been my fate. It was the only way I had of surviving. I believe that wherever you are you have seen what I have had to face and you understand why I have made these choices. At least I hope you understand.

I will tell her the truth someday, if and when I

can. I know I am weak and a poor excuse for a good son. But forgive me. I have been debating this in my mind for months. I cannot find a way right now.

So, I've decided that if Ela will have me, I will be a, a bridegroom. And then, once I know I am to be married, I will do as tradition requires. I will come and invite you to our wedding. I wish I could bring my future bride, but I cannot. So, I will travel alone to that pit at Babi Yar. To that horrific place where I hid and watched as both of you were murdered, taken from me forever, and then buried in that mass grave. And I will beg you to please attend our wedding in spirit and to give your blessing to our union. I hope you will extend your blessing.

My dear parents how I wish every day that I had done something to stop that mass murder. Please, I beg your forgiveness, but there was nothing I could do. I was just a boy alone and there were so many of them with guns. I pray you can find it in your hearts to forgive me…

Dovid's thoughts brought tears to his eyes; they trickled down his face. He knew his parents would forgive him and he also knew they would bless his marriage. They loved him that much, and Dovid knew it. The real problem lay in the fact that he, Dovid, could not forgive himself.

CHAPTER THIRTY-TWO

✡

How do you propose to a girl who is so much younger, and not only is she young but she is so beautiful? She could have her choice of men. What would she want with me? If she ever learned the truth, what then? Oskar thought as he walked to the doorway of Ela's apartment building carrying a cake he'd just purchased at the local bakery. Two days ago, when he and Ela were having lunch, she had invited him to dinner to meet her mother and her mother's friend, Artur. Oskar was nervous. For the first time, he cared about the outcome of a romantic situation. He wanted to spend the rest of his life with this girl and therefore he had to make a good impression on her mother. And to make matters worse, the mother was a strict Polish Catholic and he was a Russian soldier. Her mother would probably hate him for that alone. However, if she knew who he really was, a Jew, she might not even allow him into her home. Although he was comfortable with women, he'd never met the family of any of the girls he'd dated before. He'd avoided it at all costs. But when Ela invited him to dinner, Oskar, even as worried as he was about being rejected, had readily accepted. *I guess, no matter how unsure of myself I am, I am going to have to do this. And the worst part of it is that if I say the wrong thing it could ruin everything. I want this girl for my wife more than I have ever wanted anything in my life. And so, I must somehow find a way to make her mother like me. I have no idea how I am going to accomplish this. All I know is that I will…I must!*

CHAPTER THIRTY-THREE

✡

After an hour of being at Ela's house, Oskar realized that he had been nervous for no reason at all. Helen and her friend Artur were not judgmental of him. When he'd first walked in and handed Ela the cake, his hands had been cold and trembling. However, by the end of the evening he was playing cards with everyone and felt more at home than he had since his he was a child living at his parents' home. When he put his coat on to leave, much later than he'd originally anticipated leaving, Oskar felt the warm glow of family. At that moment, he felt safe in proposing to Ela and he was planning to do so the following evening. Ela walked him to the door.

"I had a wonderful time tonight," Oskar said. "Your mother and Artur are lovely people."

"Thank you. My mother and I are very close."

"Yes, I can see that. I can see a strong resemblance in you two." Oskar smiled, but Ela turned away. "I mean you are both so beautiful. You both have that gorgeous blond curly hair."

"Thank you," Ela said in a whisper.

"Would you have dinner with me tomorrow night? Or is it too soon? Are you busy? Do you want to wait a couple of days?"

"It's not too soon. I would love to see you tomorrow night."

"So, it's set then. I want to take you to this wonderful restaurant that I've heard a lot about."

She smiled. "I would like that."

"Eight o'clock?"

"Yes. And tomorrow, when you come to pick me up? Please feel free to knock on the door. I won't be waiting outside for you. You are now a friend of the family. You are welcome in our home anytime."

Whenever they had gone out before, Ela had

been waiting outside for Oskar. He had come to her apartment and picked her up and then after the date he'd dropped her off, but he'd never entered the building. However, now things were different. He was no longer a stranger. Oskar was a close friend who was accepted by her family.

The next day, after Oskar left work, he went to a jeweler where he purchased a ring. Then he stopped at a local tavern where he had a shot of vodka. Ela's answer to his marriage proposal would change the rest of his life. If she said no, he would be devastated. If she said yes, he would marry her under false pretenses. But he could see no other way.

After the vodka warmed his throat and gave him a quick shot of courage, he drove to Ela's apartment.

He knocked on the door and Helen let him in.

"Would you like a cup of tea before you two go to dinner?" Helen asked.

Graciously, Oskar declined. Now that he

had made up his mind about what he planned to do, he wanted to get on with it. The anxiety and anticipation of what was to come that night were overwhelming. He'd never felt so emotionally exposed. In the past, when any of his friends had said that they felt this way about a girl, Oskar would laugh. Until he met Ela, Oskar never thought he was capable of such all-encompassing love. Until Ela, he had gone through life believing that his soul had turned to steel the day he saw his parents murdered. Not that the horrors he'd witnessed made him cruel. He was still a kind and sympathetic man. That was the way his parents had raised him and he honored their ways. However, that day at Babi Yar his heart had broken into a million pieces, and once it mended he felt he would protect it and never again allow himself to care too much about anyone or anything. And then there was Ela...

There was a tiny candle of hope inside of him and with her gentle touch, she'd lit it. As their friendship grew, so did the light of that candle until it was as bright as the sun. And she had made Oskar realize that even though love came with risk, it was the greatest gift that God ever gave to man.

They sat down at a table in the restaurant; a white linen cloth covered the table.

Ela's eyes glowed in the radiance of the candlelight. Oskar decided that he'd never seen a woman as beautiful. He had planned to propose in the restaurant, but it seemed that every time he even attempted to try either the waiter or another guest walked by. He could hardly eat. By the end of dinner, he was losing his nerve. They walked to the car. He opened her door and waited until she got in. Then he walked around the other side and got behind the wheel. His mind was racing as he started the automobile.

I can't take her home without asking. If I do, I'll never find the nerve.

"Ela, would you like to come to my apartment for a cup of tea?"

She turned to look at him. He saw the disbelief in her eyes and knew that she thought he was asking her to come to his bed.

"I didn't mean to be disrespectful," he stammered. "I just…"

"Oskar, I don't know about coming to your apartment. I mean I am not sure it's a good idea …"

"Ela, I have no dishonorable intentions. The truth is that I have something to discuss with you and I couldn't talk about it in a crowded restaurant. You have my word that I will be a gentleman and will not in any way try to compromise your honor." He cleared his throat. "I just want a few minutes alone with you. To ask you a question."

"Oskar, is everything all right?"

"Yes. Please, will you trust me and come home with me?"

She shook her head. "I don't know …"

"Please, Ela."

She nodded. "All right."

Oskar's hands were trembling as he unlocked the door to his apartment. He turned on the light and ushered Ela inside.

"Won't you please sit down? Let me get you something to drink."

"It's not necessary. What is it, Oskar? You're acting so peculiar. Please, just go ahead and ask me whatever it is you want to ask," she said, but then she took a seat at the end of the sofa.

He could see that he was making her nervous. Her face was flushed and a bead of sweat had formed on her brow. He assumed she was afraid he was going to try and seduce her.

"Ela." He sat down beside her and took her hand in his. "I care for you very deeply. I think I love you." Oskar could feel the weight of the ring box in his jacket pocket. "I … I have a good position. I earn a comfortable living. As you can see I have a nice home …" He was selling himself. He couldn't believe it, but he was.

"Oskar?"

"I could give you a good life. I would be a

good husband to you."

She looked at him, her eyes wide with wonder and questions and disbelief, but he also thought he saw some form of relief in her face.

For several seconds they were both silent. Then Oskar squeezed Ela's hand. "Will you marry me?"

For several seconds the only sound was a car honking outside.

"I can't," she said and the words came out choked. "I can't."

"You don't love me?"

"I do. But I can't marry you."

"Why, Ela? Is it your mother? Is it that you don't want to leave her to live alone? She can move in here with us. I don't mind. I understand."

"No, Oskar. You don't understand at all." Ela's eyes were glassy, and Oskar was sure she was about to cry.

"Is it my age? I am too old?"

"No. No." She shook her head. Gently she freed her hand and got up and walked away from him.

"Is it my home? Do you not like it here?" His whole body was trembling now.

"Oskar. There is something you don't know about me. I never wanted to tell you because I was afraid it would change things between us. Besides that, I promised my mother I would never tell anyone."

"Ela, what is it? Please, you must trust me. You must tell me."

"I can't."

"You can. You can. Whatever it is, it doesn't matter. I love you." He could hear the desperation in his own voice.

"It will matter, Oskar."

"Please, Ela …"

"My mother. The woman you met last night…"

"Yes. Go on please."

"She isn't my birth mother. And Ela

Dobinski is not my real name. I am Eidel Weiss. My birth mother was Jewish. She had me smuggled out of the Warsaw ghetto when I was very young and sent to live with her friend Helen Dobinski and Helen's family. I am a Jew, Oskar."

Oskar's whole body was shaking. He got up and rushed over to her, taking both of his hands in hers. Tears covered his face, but he was laughing and crying at the same time.

"Ela…Eidel…I am not Oskar Ivanov. My real name is Dovid Levi. I am a Jew."

She stared into his eyes. "You're serious?"

"Yes, very serious. When I was just thirteen I watched from a hiding place as my parents were murdered by the Nazis. I escaped. My father had been a doctor in Kiev. A Russian boy he'd treated had died just the night before. I stole that boy's name, that's how I became Oskar Ivanov."

Now they were both laughing and crying in each other's arms.

"I love you, Eidel Weiss."

"I love you, Dovid Levi."

"Will you marry me under our own secret chuppah, a canopy that is visible only to us? I will break a glass, a glass that only we can see, Eidel. And we will be married, bound together forever. What do you say?"

"Yes, oh yes, Dovid Levi. I will marry you."

CHAPTER THIRTY-FOUR

✡

Oskar and Ela invited Artur and Helen out for a quiet dinner. It was over dessert and coffee that Ela told them the good news.

"Oskar and I want to get married, Mama. We hope you will give us your blessing."

"Of course, Ela." Helen's face was covered with tears as she hugged her daughter. She would miss having Ela with her all of the time but she liked Oskar and she wanted Ela to be happy and have a husband and children of her own.

Oskar went on to explain everything. He told Artur and Helen how he, Dovid Levi, had come to be Oskar Ivanov and by the time the evening ended there were no more secrets. Before they left to go home, Artur insisted on buying a round of shots to celebrate the future. Helen held Ela's hand as everyone raised their glasses to Oskar and welcomed him into their family.

Later that week, Helen went to Ela and told her that she would not be upset if Ela asked Oskar to help her find Zofia. "I will understand if you want to invite her to the wedding," Helen said.

"I don't think it's wise, Mama. The Soviet government doesn't want us looking for Jews who suffered under the Nazis. It would just point a finger at us. And as much as I would like to meet Zofia, you are my real mother and you are the one whom I want to be at my wedding. I think perhaps it is best that we leave well enough alone."

"You know I love you, Ela, and I would do anything for you."

"I do know that, Mama. In fact, I am worried about you. Will you be all right once I move out of our home? You know I will come to see you often."

"I will be all right. I have Artur. He will visit me…"

"Are you sure, Mama? You look so sad."

"I am sure," Helen said mustering a smile. The truth was that she would miss Ela desperately. But over the last few years, she had begun to worry that Ela would be an old maid. And quite frankly, her greatest concern was that Ela would be alone when she got older after Helen passed away. Now, Helen could rest easy. Ela would have a life besides the life she shared with her mother.

Helen was surprised at Ela's decision not to search for Zofia, but she agreed that it was for the best. No one knew that Ela and Oskar were Jewish. Why shine a light on a fact that could change the course of their lives in a negative way? Right now, things were good for them. They were a young couple just starting out. Oskar had a good paying job and Ela was working too. Both of them were easily accepted by others. They would have no problems with the Soviets because of Oskar. Yes, Ela was right. Best to leave well enough alone.

CHAPTER THIRTY-FIVE

✡

Helen and Artur went out for dinner as they always did the following Wednesday evening. They went to the same small café and sat across from each other. However, since they'd received the news about Ela and Oskar getting married, Helen had begun to feel sad about living alone. Ela was going to be moving in with Oskar right after the wedding. Helen had never been by herself for a long period of time. And although she would never tell Ela, she was a little frightened by the idea. And, perhaps it was her fault, but even though she and Artur had become good friends, a true romance had never sparked between them. They had spent a night or two in each other's arms, but more for comfort than out of passion or true love. Still, with everything changing so quickly in Helen's life, she now considered discussing marriage with Artur. He had been living by himself since Maci's death. He occasionally mentioned how hard it was for a man living alone. Sometimes, when he came to pick her up, his clothes were not exactly clean and he looked a little disheveled. Artur seemed to relish coming to Helen's house for a home-cooked meal. To marry a good friend was not so bad, she thought. After all, she had once been with the great love of her life. If Artur would agree to marry her, they would both have companions.

They walked home from the restaurant side by side. It was a cold night. Helen pulled her coat tightly around her.

"I don't know how to ask you this," Helen said.

"Ask me anything? Why not?" He smiled, his breath coming out white. "What do you need? Money?"

"Not money," she said. "Ela is getting married, as you know." She stuttered. "I...oh Artur. How am I going to say this to you? I guess what I am trying to say is that I am going to be very lonely. You live alone. Sometimes you are lonely too, yes?"

"Very. Very lonely. You have filled my life since Maci died. I cherish our friendship," he said. "I think I know what you want to say. I will say it for you. Perhaps we should get married? You and I?"

"Yes, I was thinking that perhaps it would be good for both of us." She smiled.

He took her hand. "So," he smiled and patted her hand. "Then, let's do it."

"Yes, lets." She looked up at him and her face lit up.

CHAPTER THIRTY-SIX

✡

The following morning Ela was at work when one of the bosses came out of his office and walked over to her.

"Ela Dobinski?"

"Yes." She sat up straight. The bosses rarely came over and called for the secretaries by name. *I hope I didn't do something wrong on that letter that I just put into the box of finished work,* she thought.

"There is a phone call for you. You can pick it up in my office."

"A phone call?"

The boss nodded. "Go on. Quickly, there is work to be done."

Ela got up and went into the office.

"This is Ela Dobinski," she said.

Then her face went white. She passed out and fell to the ground.

CHAPTER THIRTY-SEVEN

✡

Early that same morning after Ela left for work, Helen got ready to go to the bus stop. She had recently changed jobs and needed to take two buses to get to her new place of employment, a garment factory. Although she'd loved working at the school, the pay at the factory was significantly better. An icy wind whipped her hair away from her face as she waited at the bus stop with a large group of others who took the bus to work each day.

Her thoughts were of the future. She liked Artur well enough, and she was glad he was in her life. But change was always hard to accept.

I should be used to it. My life has always been filled with change. And, God knows, I want my Ela to be happy. But I am going to miss the little world she and I have shared all these years. Of course, Ela will still come to visit with Oskar at least once a week. But things will never be the same.

It was never going to be just mother and daughter ever again. Helen would not tell Ela, but this made her terribly depressed.

When Helen arrived at work, she signed in and raced to her machine. Her quota had to be met for the day, so she began to work quickly. Her fingers were still stiff from the cold. It took a few minutes for them to become nibble. But she was used to that; it was always that way in the winter. However, today, her mind was distracted by thoughts of the past, the present, and the uncertain future. Helen remembered Ela, the way she was as a child. Memories of the little girl trickled through her mind like tiny raindrops. She even had a visual recollection of the night that the man from the underground had brought Ela to her from the ghetto. He had pushed the sleeping Ela into Helen's arms. Helen could still remember the innocent pale eyelids flickering as Ela slept. She recalled how she knew, even then, at that very first moment, that she would sacrifice everything she had to protect the poor little girl who needed her so desperately.

"Ela," Helen whispered. "Things are going to change for us. And, even though I have lived with it all of my life, I am so afraid of change…"

Just then Helen felt a tug on her hair. At first it was just a gentle pull, but then it grew stronger. She felt the strands of her hair being ripped out of her head as the machine tangling her hair drew more and more of it inside. The hair wrapped around her neck, tearing and strangling as it yanked at her head. Although it seemed like hours, all of this happened within seconds. The machine was swallowing her up like a starving steel giant. At first, Helen screamed in terror. When Helen had been hired she'd been warned that she must be careful around the machine. "The machine is a demon. I swear it is alive. Take heed, Helen. It's always watching and waiting for its operator to make a mistake. Don't let it be you," the woman who trained her had said. And usually, she was very cautious. But today she had let her guard down. Somehow she had forgotten the warning. She'd been distracted and the machine had been waiting. The woman who trained her was right. And now the machine had taken on a life of its own. It had her in its grip and refused to release her until it broke her neck.

The rest of the workers gathered at her station. Some were trying to pull her free but without success. The screams of her co-workers were louder than the machines that were roaring all around her but human power was weaker. The machine stood like Goliath, its very heart of cold metal filled with the desire to destroy her, to swallow her up. Helen felt tears fall on her face. She could hear the others wailing and hollering all around her. But then … the sound stopped. Then … there was only silence.

Helen saw a white shimmering light. At first, it was right in front of her. Then it surrounded her entire body. The pain was gone in an instant and she felt no fear. Then, out of nowhere, she saw Eryk walking towards her. He reached out his hands to her.

"Eryk," she said. Her voice was barely a

whisper.

"Helen, my darling, my love. I have been waiting patiently for a very long time for you to come to me. And now you're here in my arms. My God, Helen, I love you."

"Eryk, is it really you?"

"It's me. Come with me, Helen. Come home with me. I have missed you so much. You are and have always been my one true love."

She fell into his arms. He kissed her. The taste of his lips, the smell of his skin, the brush of his hair against her cheek. It was all just as perfect as she remembered it.

"But what will become of Ela if I go with you?"

"She will be fine. Dovid Levi is a good man. I have been watching over both of you. I know that he will take care of her. Now it's time for you and me to be together for eternity. We have both suffered far too much. Come with me Helen … Come, let's go home."

"Eryk. I am here with you now. Take me home."

He took her hand. She felt a warm glow come over her. "I have missed you too, my love. Every day since you've been gone, I've missed you," she said as they walked into the light, hand in hand.

CHAPTER THIRTY-EIGHT

✡

Ela's eyes opened slowly. It was dark in her bedroom. Oskar was sitting on a chair at her side. She could hear faint sounds of traffic outside her window.

"Oskar, my Mother?"

In the shadows from the moonlight that filtered through the window, she saw him nod. "I'm sorry, Ela."

"She's dead? Oskar, she's really gone? Is it true?"

He swept her into his arms and held her. "Yes, I am sorry." He spoke in a whisper, his voice cracking as he felt her pain transfer from her heart into his.

"Oskar. I can't go on without my mother. I can't."

"I will be here with you forever, Ela. You will be my wife, my best friend. I can't take away your misery, but I can hold you and share it with you."

"Every place I go, I will see her memory. The shops, the streets, the school, the subway." Ela was weeping. "This apartment. She told me stories here in this bedroom. Bible stories when I was just a child. I can't stay here in Warsaw without her."

He held Ela in his arms while she cried, kissing her forehead.

"I have some money put away. Let's leave here. If we declare our Judaism we can get out of Poland and go to Israel."

"I don't know about Israel. There is such unrest there."

"Yes, that's true. So, what do you think about this?" He hesitated and touched her cheek, wiping a tear away with his thumb. "As I said, I have some money put away. We can go to Israel and then from there we can get into America. Once we are in America, I will find work."

"America? Oskar, can you speak any

English?"

"I can get by. I learned during the war."

"I don't speak much English at all. I took a class once. But I don't speak it well enough to live there. I hardly speak Russian."

"You do very well with Russian, between the little bit of Polish I speak and the little bit of Russian you speak we are getting married." He smiled, trying to make her laugh.

"You speak perfect Polish," she said. But she couldn't laugh at his joke, her heart was breaking with the loss of her dearest friend, her mother. "You do speak perfect Polish. I speak a little Russian," she corrected him.

"I speak pretty good English, too. I suppose I am good at learning languages. Don't worry, I'll teach you English."

"America?"

"Yes. America, a place where we can be accepted as Jews."

"Where did you get all this money?"

"Let's just say, I wasn't always a good

person. I did what I had to do."

"You took bribes."

"Ela, I did what I had to do to survive. Do you really want to know all the details? I don't think you do. Do you know that I love you and that I would do anything for you?"

"Yes, I do know that, Oskar."

"Then, please, let that be enough."

"My mother, the arrangements for her funeral. Someone has to call Artur."

"Everything is done. I have taken care of everything."

"Sleep here beside me," she said. "Hold me in your arms. I can't bear to be alone tonight."

"I'll stay with you. I will keep you safe in my arms and comfort you, but I will not make love to you until we say our vows. I believe that my parents are watching. In their honor, I would like to wait until you are my wife."

She nuzzled closer to him.

Then he continued. "If you want to leave Poland with me after the funeral I'll make arrangements for us to go. We can get married in the United States. But there is something I must do before we leave."

"What is it, Oskar?"

"I must go back to Kiev; to the outskirts—to the ravine at Babi Yar. Will you come with me? I want to invite my parents to our wedding. In the Jewish tradition, when a couple is going to wed they go to the cemetery to invite their dead loved ones to come to the wedding. My parents are buried in a mass grave at Babi Yar. So, I will go there and ask them to attend our wedding."

"Yes, I will go with you, Oskar. I want to go with you."

"We will invite your mother, too."

"Yes, let's do that," she said, squeezing his arm. "I can't believe she will not be at my side on my wedding day. Oskar, it hurts me so much."

"I know, I know. I wish she could be with us in the flesh. But she will be with us in spirit as will my parents."

"It is the best we can do. From now on, we will have only each other," Ela said.

"Yes. I wish I had the power to bring her back to you, but I don't, my darling. All I have to offer is my eternal love and devotion. If I could, I would do anything to see you smile."

"I know that, Oskar. Is there anything I can do for you? Is there anything that would make you happy?" Ela asked.

A face from the past appeared in Oskar's mind. It was the face of that man from the concentration camp, Moishe Finkelstein. "Go to America." Oskar could see Finkelstein's face and hear the message that had been given him. "Go to America."

"It would mean so much to me if we could be married under a chuppah by a rabbi. I miss the traditions I grew up with. I long to sign my name as Dovid Levi and to see your name beside mine signed as Eidel Weiss. Between the Nazis and the Soviets, I have endured so much anti-Semitism. I've hidden my birthright in shame. It was the only way to survive. I am not proud of what I did. A better man would have died for what he believed in. But I am a coward, Ela. I wanted to live."

"I am glad you chose to live," she said.

"If you will agree, I would prefer to leave the names of Ela and Oskar here in Europe. From the day we land on American soil I would like to openly accept our Jewish heritage and to go by the names of Dovid and Eidel."

"If this is what you want, this is what we will do," Ela said. It didn't matter to her. She knew almost nothing about Judaism. However, she was willing to try to learn if it made him happy.

"I've always wanted to go back and live the life my parents intended for me. The life the Rabbi described to me on the day of my Bar Mitzvah. Every time I've witnessed the persecution of our people I have always wanted to openly say, 'I am a Jew' and be proud of my family, of my background and who I am. But I have never been able to do that in Poland or in Russia. From the day the Nazis marched into Kiev I began to live a lie.

Do you know that when I was in the army I had to hide my circumcision? I was afraid someone would see it and learn the truth that I am a Jew. I want to smash that lie, Ela."

"Then…we will smash it together."

CHAPTER THIRTY-NINE

✡

1957

Ela sold most of the furniture in Helen's apartment. She gave a few special pieces to Helen's good friend who lived upstairs. She also called Artur and invited him over. When he arrived, she gave him back an emerald ring that he had given her mother. Artur stayed with Ela and Dovid for several hours talking about how much he would miss Helen.

"Your mother was very brave. You should be proud," Artur said. "During the Nazi occupation, she worked to help the resistance. I worked with them too. That is how I know of her bravery. And you know as well as I do what a small and delicate creature she was. In her youth, her beauty was unsurpassed. I will tell you that much is for sure." He smiled. "You look just like her, Ela," he said.

Everyone always said I looked just like my

mother, Helen. How was that possible when she wasn't my birth mother? When I asked my mother about it she said it was God's way of saving me. Because I looked just like her, no one questioned whether she was my mother. But she had so many secrets. And I still have so many unanswered questions. Who was the man in the resistance who gave her the Star of David necklace to give to me? Helen said he got it from Zofia Weiss, but how was it that he knew both my mother and Zofia? Was he my father? But Helen said that my birth father was an American who abandoned Zofia when she got pregnant. Where is this American? What happened to him? I just have so many questions, Helen thought, while Artur was still speaking.

Artur went on, "And one thing was for certain, your mother hated the Nazis and so she fought against them in any way she could. Your father, who was a good friend of mine, didn't know that she was a part of the resistance until later. He would have strongly forbidden it. But she didn't care. Helen was like a small package of beautiful dynamite. She had the courage of a lion."

"Artur…can I ask you a question, please?"

"Yes, of course, Ela. Anything."

"My mother gave me a necklace. A Star of David that she said you brought to her. She said you got it from a man who was in the resistance. Do you know anything more about this necklace? Do you know who the man was? Do you know what his relationship with my mother was? And do you know anything about who he got the necklace from?"

Artur looked away and walked over to the window. He glanced outside and for a long moment, he was silent. Dovid watched him carefully.

Artur stood staring outside. He was lost in thought. *How much does Ela know already? How much would Helen want me to tell her? I can't bring myself to soil Helen's memory in Ela's heart. I dare not mention Eryk and the fact that he and Helen were lovers. And what does she know already about the necklace? I think it is best if I say I have no knowledge of anything. That way I will stay true to Helen and never reveal any secrets even though she is gone. If there is something*

Helen wanted Ela to know, she would have told her. It is not my place to share any secrets.

"I am afraid I don't know anything."

"But my mother said that it was you who brought her the necklace. The man from the resistance gave it to you to give to her. I am assuming he must have been a mutual friend of both of yours. You must know something about him?"

Artur swallowed hard and shook his head. "He was in the resistance. But I hardly knew him. I wouldn't call him a mutual friend. I don't know why he wanted me to give the necklace to your mother or where he got it. He gave it to me as the Nazis were taking him to be executed. They hung him in the middle of town. I had only a moment to speak with him. He slipped the necklace into my hand as they were dragging him away. He didn't have a chance to tell me anything except that he wanted me to give the necklace to your mother."

"Executed for what? What did he do?"

"He started a fire in the home of a high-ranking Nazi official. The whole family died. But he got caught."

"What was his name?"

"Eryk Jawoski."

"I never heard my mother mention his name. Never. It's all so strange and confusing, isn't it?"

"Yes. Very," Artur said. "But it is best to let the past go, Ela. There are no answers to these questions. Things happened during the war. Things no one can explain. All you need to know is that your mother loved you very much. And that she was a wonderful woman." He was referring to Helen but Ela wondered if he knew about Zofia Weiss.

"You loved her, didn't you?"

"Yes, I did. When we were young she was a good friend to me and my wife. Then, after my wife died, she was a comfort to me. Although we were never madly in love, I did love her."

"I know you did, Artur."

After Artur left, Eidel sat down on one of the chairs that were still left in the almost empty apartment. "He still calls me Ela." She smiled sadly at Dovid.

"I know. And until we leave Poland, all of your old friends and neighbors will call you Ela," Dovid said.

"The name will always hold a special place in my heart. It's what my mother called me."

"I know, and I understand. You can keep it if you'd like. I will call you Ela if you prefer."

"No, Dovid. I want you to call me Eidel. I want to leave Poland and the war behind me."

Dovid insisted that Eidel keep all of the money she made from the sale of Helen's things. As they were cleaning out the drawers, they found a small cloth purse. Inside, Helen had left a nice sum of money. She had lived meagerly her entire life, working first at the school and then at the factory. When Eidel showed Dovid the money and tried to give it to him he said, "This money belongs to you, Eidel. It is from your mother. She would have wanted you to have it. I won't take it from you. We are doing all right. I have plenty and I can always work. Hold onto the cash you have in case you ever need anything."

"But we are going to be married. I want to share everything I have with you. You are sharing everything with me," she said.

"I know. But I am a man and I'm old-fashioned. A man takes care of his wife. His wife doesn't take care of him."

"But if it turns out that we need it?"

"If we need it, we'll use it. But if not, and I really hope not, you just hold on to it," Dovid said.

Eidel packed a suitcase with her personal things and a few meaningful pieces that had belonged to Helen. As she was going through Helen's closet and deciding what to take, she came across the wedding dress Zofia had made for Helen's wedding. Eidel took it out of the closet. It had yellowed a bit, but it was apparent that the workmanship was very professional. Each pearl had been stitched carefully into the fabric by hand. Eidel held one of the pearls in her palm and thought, *Zofia Weiss also held this pearl in her fingers while she sewed it into this gown. How beautiful my mother must have looked. She was so young then, and the Nazis had not yet ruined Poland. And how odd, that she and Zofia had been such dear friends. They were so close that Zofia had not only made this dress but she had also made the quilt that my mother kept on her bed. It was a wedding gift.*

They had such a short time together. However, because of me, even though they only saw each other one more time, they were bound together for life. Eidel held the gown up to her face trying to smell the essence of her mother and the past. But the gown was old and nothing lingered.

I will take this dress with me and I'll wear it when Dovid and I are married. My mother would have wanted that. And I know she will be looking down from Heaven and see me wearing it as I walk down the aisle. And as she is watching she will know how much I love her and how much I wish she could share my wedding day with me.

Eidel felt the tears sting her eyes as she packed the dress. Then she walked over to the quilt that lay on her mother's bed and picked it up. This time, when she held it to her face, she could feel her mother's presence. She folded it and put it in her suitcase. The woman upstairs would be sending her husband to take the bed later that day. Eidel wished she could bring it with her. It held so many memories but it was impossible to take a bed onboard a ship.

Dovid was twenty-nine and Eidel was seventeen when they left Warsaw. Together, hand in hand, they boarded a ship headed to Israel. They planned to wait there for their visas to be approved to enter the United States of America. In 1948, the U.S.A. passed the Displaced Persons Act, making it easier for Jews to enter the United States. They could have waited for their visas in Poland, but Dovid was leery of the Communists. He didn't trust the regime not to turn on them and stop the Jews from leaving. "Let's get out while we can. They are letting us go now. We will be safe waiting in Israel," he told Eidel.

The day that Ela and Oskar boarded that ship they ceased to exist and Dovid and Eidel were reborn.

The ship was a crowded, smelly, messy place. It was the middle of summer and the sun beat down on the deck relentlessly. During the middle of the day, the heat was unbearable. Many days, Eidel became seasick, vomiting from the heat or from the arrival of a storm that kicked up waves, tossing the boat around in the ocean like a toy. It was a ship filled with the survivors of Hitler's terrible reign. People who had seen and suffered unimaginable horrors. Men and women who had lost everything they had, their loved ones, their homes, their careers, and any material possessions they had once owned. But even so, many were very grateful to be alive. Dovid, with his contagious laugh and relaxed manner, made friends easily. Eidel, however, was too depressed from the loss of her mother to talk to anyone. She kept to herself most of the time, staying in her bed. Dovid tried to include her in card games with people who spoke Polish. He was hoping that it would bring her out of her shell. But she always begged off and went to sit on the deck alone. Dovid followed her the first time she went off by herself and tried to sit with her. However, she asked him to leave her alone for a while. She said she needed the time to mourn her mother. He respected her wishes and let her be. *Some of this is her age,* he reminded himself. *She is so very young and all of this is so very foreign to her. My little Eidel is like a delicate rose. I have to take tender care of her. Sometimes I wonder what such a beautiful young girl would want with an old man like me.*

The ship was overcrowded to the point of being uncomfortable. However, the atmosphere onboard was one of great hope and the promise of a future free from fear in a Jewish homeland. The birth of Israel brought a new-found strength to a people who had been persecuted through the ages. Those fortunate enough to be aboard this vessel openly discussed the fact that they knew they had survived in order to carry on their Jewish heritage. Even so, there was plenty of survivor guilt amongst those who had lived while so many had died. Many times, cries could be heard during the night coming from those suffering from nightmares. But in spite of all that was lost, there was also joy, singing and dancing, and talk of the children who would be born under the flag of the Jewish people. They were proud of the blue and white flag of Israel. When someone started a sing-a-long, Eidel sat on the sidelines trying to clap with them but she looked like she felt out of place. They often sang songs of freedom in Yiddish, or large groups would get together and begin to pray and give thanks for their survival. But the prayers were always in Hebrew. First of all, she didn't know any Yiddish or Hebrew and second, although she was alive and grateful to have Dovid at her side, she was still devastated by her mother's death and thought about Helen constantly. Quite frankly, she was not feeling very joyful.

While they were aboard the ship, Dovid made friends with a survivor who had been a part of the resistance in France. He told Dovid that when he got to Israel he planned to live on a kibbutz in Tiberius, and he asked Dovid to bring Eidel and join him. Dovid and Eidel hadn't made any plans as to where they would go when they arrived, so when the ship docked in Israel they rode several busses to the kibbutz in Tiberius. It was a beautiful piece of land, with silver-leafed olive trees that shimmered in the bright sunlight. There were orchards of red apples and fields of growing crops. The main building where everyone gathered for meals was large with ample seating and a huge kitchen where the food preparation took place. The kibbutz was located on a mountain overlooking the Sea of Galilee. To Dovid, it felt like he had died and gone to Heaven. He loved his homeland and he loved the kibbutz where there was no rent to be paid or food to be bought. No money exchanged hands. Instead, each member had a job to do to earn his keep. During the day, everyone worked together, growing crops, cooking, sewing, and teaching and carrying for the children. What they couldn't grow or produce on their own, they traded for. Most nights after dinner, someone would pull out a guitar and everyone sang along.

Because they did not have to spend money to live on the kibbutz, Dovid was able to save the money that he had left over after paying for their passage on the ship. He would need this money to start his new life with Eidel when they got to America.

Friday nights and Saturday afternoons were very special times on the kibbutz. This was the Sabbath, the holiest of days in Jewish law.. It began on Friday at sundown, when all the members gathered to share shared a candlelit, ceremonious Shabbat dinner. Hebrew prayers were sung by a man who had been a cantor in Germany before the war. He had survived two horrific transports in cattle cars where he was stuffed in and forced to stand for days because there was no room to sit. He told everyone how he'd seen the very young and very old perish quickly from the heat.

Everyone else suffered. Some died of thirst but some made it through. After each transport, he survived several perilous years in concentration camps. "I came close to death more times than I can count. Each time, an unexpected miracle occurred that allowed me to live. I know that I am alive because God has a purpose for me. And so, I sing praises to him." He told them. Although his hair had turned white and he looked far older than his age, his voice was still as pure and sweet as sap from a sugar maple tree. The Sabbath celebration lasted until sundown on Saturday. The entire day was a day of rest. No work was to be done during the Sabbath. This was a period dedicated to the enjoyment and appreciation of God's gifts of friends, and loved ones. It was also a time of reflection and a time to remember God's grace and rejoice in his glory.

Eidel tried to fit in but she couldn't. She was so self-conscious of everything she did. She always felt like an outsider at the kibbutz. She had never learned anything about Judaism and she felt that people expected her to know things. After all, she was Jewish. But she didn't know anything or anyone and so she didn't speak or let anyone get too close to her. It would have been difficult to explain what had happened in her life. How she had been raised Catholic and how she hadn't known anything about being Jewish until she was a teenager. So, although she was present in body, she gave the impression of being aloof. And because of this, people left her alone.

A day never passed that Eidel didn't think about her mother. Many times, she also thought about Zofia Weiss. She had so many mixed feelings about the woman who had given her life, and she had so many unanswered questions.

Do you ever think about me, Zofia Weiss? Or did you just forget me when I was taken out of the ghetto? Was it easy for you to put me out of your mind and just get on with your life? Did you really give me up for my sake like Helen said you did or was it just easier to survive without a child to care for?

These questions plagued Eidel's mind and yet, Eidel had no idea where to begin to look for Zofia. Sometimes she wondered if she would really have wanted to find her. She wasn't sure she wanted answers to those painful questions. However, unbeknownst to Eidel, Zofia Weiss was not far away. She was living on a kibbutz with her husband and adopted daughter only ten miles away. Unbeknownst to Eidel, Zofia had never stopped thinking of her. Memories of Eidel and thoughts of seeing her again were all that kept Zofia alive during the suffering she endured under the Nazi occupation. If Zofia ever had the chance to talk to Eidel, she would have told Eidel that she had loved her more than her own life.

CHAPTER FOURTY

✡

Dovid took a day away from the kibbutz and went into town to buy wedding rings, and he and Ediel were married in a simple ceremony on the kibbutz. Rabbi Gutelman, who performed the ceremony, was a concentration camp survivor who lost his entire family. Dovid's parents' dream that he would be married under a chuppah, a canopy, was fulfilled. All of the members of the kibbutz built a chuppah from wooden posts and decorated it with flowers. They set it up outside in an open field and everyone gathered around to watch the wedding. Dovid borrowed a suit from one of the men with whom he had made friends in the kibbutz. It didn't fit him well; he was too muscular and it looked too small. But he wore it proudly as he stood at the altar, trembling with joy and anticipation. One of the members of the kibbutz played the violin. He finished his song and then hesitated. For a moment, the entire crowd was silent. Then Eidel came walking toward Dovid. She looked radiant in her beaded wedding gown—the gown Helen had worn on her wedding day. The gown Zofia Weiss had painstakingly beaded by hand. Neither of Eidel's mothers was present in body but both were a part of her wedding day.

As Dovid watched Eidel walking toward him, his thoughts turned to his parents. *How I wish you could both be here and know the wonderful, beautiful girl who is about to be my kallah, my bride. How I wish you could both see this; you would be so proud. Today, I am a chosson, a bridegroom. Papa, I want you to rest in peace and know that I will have a son. When he is born, I will name him for you. The Levi name will not be lost.*

As they said their vows, Dovid could feel the heat of his father's hand on his shoulder and the gentle brush of his mother's kiss on his cheek, and he knew that they were there with him on that very special day. And so it was that as the Sea of Galilee sparkled like tiny diamonds bathed in the rays of the setting sun, and as the sky turned to shades of lavender and plum, Ela Dobinsky became Eidel Levi.

Dovid placed the ring on Eidel's finger and repeated after the rabbi, "Behold, you are consecrated to me with this ring according to the laws of Moses and Israel."

***

Dovid and Eidel made love until dawn. He was tender and not only was it a sexually satisfying experience for Eidel, but it was also a bonding of two beings in body and in spirit. In the early hours of the morning, when they were both spent, he turned to her and whispered, "Now we are one person. We are one soul. For the rest of our lives, I will live to protect you from harm. I will provide for you the very best that I can. And you can always come to me no matter what you need and I will try to give it to you."

She began to cry. "I love you, Dovi. But sometimes I miss my mother so much. I am lost here in this strange country. I feel so different from everyone else."

"I know you do. And I know that you don't realize it, but everyone here on the kibbutz likes you."

"They speak in Yiddish. They make jokes about their mothers' special Jewish recipes and they talk about how they grew up and celebrated strange holidays like Purim and Sukkot. I don't know anything about these things. My mother never made anything called gefilte fish. I just always feel like I never know what to say to anyone."

"You have me, Eidel. You will always have me. I love you just as you are. You don't have to change one thing about yourself. In fact, I would be very angry if you did," he said touching her chin. Then he added, "Before you know it, we will be going to America. There you will find people of all religions. You won't feel so out of place. You'll find it easier to fit in."

Dovid loved the kibbutz. If it had been his choice, they would have stayed forever. He felt connected to the very soil of Israel. He took great pride in the land. It reminded him of growing up with his parents. He loved the sound of Yiddish. His mother had often spoken to him in Yiddish and when he heard the women chatting away it brought back sweet memories. Dovid kibitzed, he joked with the men, talking about nothing of any importance, but feeling a part of a larger whole that was more important than just himself. The hard work outside in the fields stretched his muscles and he slept well at night. But even though he loved living on the kibbutz in Israel, it was easy to see that his wife was not adjusting well to Jewish life. And Dovid adored his Eidel. Dovid understood her in a way he had never understood anyone else. He forgave her for eventually taking him away from the country he loved because he loved her even more than he loved Israel. Still, their visas did not come and they would have to continue to wait. And so he decided to try and make her happy by taking her to a very special place he had heard about from one of his friends on the kibbutz. The friend's name was Ari, and he was a Sabra, born and raised in Israel. He was the first person on the kibbutz to offer his hand in friendship to Dovid. As they got to know one another, Dovid learned that he and Ari had a great deal in common. Ari, too, had been a soldier. He'd fought in the War of Independence and was fiercely devoted to Israel. They discussed what it had been like for them as soldiers. They admitted that they shared the fear of dying and that they had both hid their fears behind a brave front during battle. Each of them could still recall the smell of sulfur from the gunpowder and the wicked odor of iron that rose out of the pools of spilled blood on the battlefield. Ari had never married. He had been in love once, he said, but he claimed to enjoy his freedom too much to ever sign his name on a marriage license. Still, he understood when Dovid told him how much he loved Eidel. Dovid also told Ari that he was waiting for their visas to the U.S. and how he wished that Eidel wanted to stay in Israel instead of going to America. That was when Ari came up with the idea of a day trip to surprise Eidel. Ari went ahead and arranged for both Dovid and Eidel to take the day off from working at the kibbutz. Then he gave Dovid very explicit directions to their destination and also told him exactly what to look for when he got there.

"I asked my friend if you could use his car. He said yes, but to be careful. By the way, can you drive?"

"Yes, I can," Dovid said.

"Good. You'll use the car," Ari said. He then told Dovid a wonderful story about the place he was sending them. "When you get there, tell her the story," he said. Then added, "Once she hears this story she will fall in love with Israel too. After all, it is a very magical land."

"Get dressed," Dovid said to Eidel, early in the morning on the day of the trip. "I have somewhere very special that I want to take you."

Eidel turned over in bed. She stretched like a cat and looked into his eyes. "Where?" she asked, still half-asleep.

"Somewhere I think you are going to enjoy. We are going off the kibbutz today. And, not only that, but I also have a magical story to tell you when we get there." He smiled and winked.

"They are expecting me to work in the kitchen today," she said. "I can't go." She hated the chopping and cooking that was required of her. It was backbreaking and exhausting. And again, all the women in the kitchen spoke in Hebrew or Yiddish. However, she understood that everyone had to do his or her job in order for the kibbutz to work. It was a communal farm where everyone pitched in and did their share. She would never tell Dovid but she couldn't wait until they left the kibbutz.

"I took care of it. I already made arrangements for us to take today off. It's sort of like our honeymoon day. You will really like what I have planned. I promise. But you must dress very modestly."

"What do you mean modestly? Don't I always?"

"Well, not like this. You are really going to have to dress modestly. Do you have a long skirt?"

"You mean tea-length?"

"No, longer—to cover your ankles. You must be sure your arms and your chest are covered as well. Your shirt should come down below your elbows and your top should cover you up to your collarbone."

"I have a blouse but I don't have a long skirt like that. Why would I need one?"

"We're going to a very religious section. The dress code is specific."

"I don't want to go," she said. "It makes me nervous. I won't fit in."

"You'll love it. I won't fit in either. But it will be a beautiful day. Do you trust me?"

"Of course, Dovid. I married you."

"Then relax. This is going to be wonderful. I'll go and see if I can borrow a long skirt for you from one of the other women," he said. Then he got up out of bed and left their room.

Ten minutes passed and Dovid returned carrying a long gray cotton skirt in his hands.

Eidel looked at him skeptically. "Are you sure we should do this?" She thought the skirt was hideous, but she didn't say so because he was so excited that she didn't want to spoil things.

"Absolutely." He smiled and handed her the skirt. "Also, make sure you are wearing low-heeled shoes. We are going to do some walking. Hiking, really. It's sort of like a nature walk."

"Really, Dovid? I have never done a hike in my life. Isn't that something you did in the army? This is very strange."

"Yes, we had to do it in the army. But this is different. We are going somewhere special. Come on, no more questions. You'll love it. I promise."

Something in his eyes soothed her. It was frightening for her to be in this strange place, and now she was going to an even stranger place, but she loved her husband and so she mustered a laugh. "All right. Let's go," she said.

Eidel got dressed. She wore a long-sleeve white shirt, buttoned all the way up to the top of her neck, and the long gray skirt. She put on a pair of kitten heels. She felt matronly and odd. Once she was ready to leave she turned to Dovid and said, "I look really strange, don't I?"

"You can never be anything but beautiful in my eyes," he said. "But I am afraid that your shoes aren't low-heeled enough. You should be wearing flat shoes today."

As if this doesn't look bad enough, she thought. But she put on an old pair of flats that she wore to work in the kitchen. *I look really terrible and these shoes don't help.*

"I look really bad, Dovid. Do you think people will stare at me?"

"No. I think you will be dressed appropriately for where we are going. I've borrowed a car so I can drive us there."

"Do you know how to drive?"

"I learned in the army. Come, let's get going. We'll have fun."

They stopped at the kibbutz kitchen to have a quick breakfast of hummus, vegetables, and hard-boiled eggs before they left. Eidel had never told Dovid, but the food at the kibbutz was not appealing to her. Besides that, the people on the kibbutz did something called 'keep kosher' and she was always afraid she would accidentally break some serious dietary law. They never ate dairy and meat at the same meal. In fact, they had two sets of dishes, one to be used for dairy, the other for meat. Shellfish and pork were not allowed at all. And they had all kinds of other rules that Eidel didn't understand. When she was growing up, if Helen was able to get milk she would insist Eidel drink it regardless of what else they were able to get to eat. Not that meat was readily available, but when it was she ate it with or without a glass of milk. During the war, Eidel ate whatever Helen could provide including pork. She felt blessed when Helen brought home pork sausages. However, before she came to Israel she had never eaten raw vegetables in the morning. And the spices the women used in their cooking tasted odd to her too. But she never told Dovid and he seemed to like the food. This morning, as she sat across from her beloved husband at the table, she smiled at him, wanting to please him, and so she forced herself to eat the oddly-flavored chickpea paste with the green peppers and carrots.

After they finished eating they were on their way. They traveled north, through a beautiful mountainous terrain. Dovid pulled over and stopped the car. He got out and opened Eidel's door. He took her hand.

"I want you to see something," he said, as he led her through a narrow grassy area to a low-lying body of water with large gray stones that were above the water level. In order to cross, one had to carefully walk from stone to stone without falling. Eidel was having trouble keeping her balance. She was trembling as she looked at Dovid.

"I think we should go back," she said,

tripping on a slippery rock. He caught her before she fell.

"You'll be all right. Don't be afraid. Just lean on me. I won't let you fall, Eidel," he said. Her feet were unsteady on the slippery rocks and so he was practically carrying her. Then he stopped, looked into her eyes, and added, "I will never let you fall. I won't let you fall here in this river and I won't let you fall in life. No matter what happens, I will always be with you to catch you if you start to slip. This is my vow to you."

"You're very poetic today," she said, smiling at him and winking but still holding on to him tightly.

"Can you hear that?" he asked.

"What?"

"It's running water."

"Yes, now that you mention it I can. It's stronger than this river."

"Exactly. It's much stronger and it's only a little further. Your special surprise is very close now," he said. They walked over several more stones and then the mountains parted and before them stood a magnificent waterfall.

"Oh Dovi, it is beautiful," Eidel gasped, turning her head toward him. He held her in his arms so she wouldn't slide on the slippery patches.

"Look over there," he said pointing. "There is a rainbow in the waterfall. Do you see it?" He kissed her hair.

"I do. I see it, Dovi."

"That rainbow is a symbol of our future together. Our lives will be filled with joyous colors. This I promise you, my wife, my own, my Eidel Levi."

She turned to look at him and fell into his arms. There was no one around. He began kissing her and the passion overtook them. They made love with the wild roar of the waterfall in the background and a vivid rainbow shining over them.

Afterward, they lay on the ground looking up at the clouds. "Did you ever look at clouds when you were a child and imagine that they were monsters or dogs or witches?"

"I did," Dovid said.

"Me too." She squeezed his hand. "Look at that one. It looks like a dragon."

"You're right. But he looks like a friendly dragon," Dovid said.

"What if he's not?" Eidel wondered wistfully.

"Then I will slay him for you like a knight would do for his princess."

"You would, huh? But you have already won my hand. What is at stake now if you slay the dragon?"

"Your love, my princess. I will spend a lifetime fighting dragons to keep your love."

She leaned over and kissed him. He held her in his arms and sighed. He had never cared so much for another person in his entire life.

The sun was high in the sky and Dovid knew from the sun's position that it was getting close to noon.

"We should go," he whispered in her ear.

"Even though I hate to leave this place."

"I know, me too," she said.

He stood up and then helped her to her feet and together they walked back toward the car. When they were almost there, Dovid stopped and turned to Eidel.

"Just look around you, Eidel. This land belongs to our people. They fought and died for it. For centuries, Jews have been treated like a pariah in every country in the world. But now we have a homeland of our own. This is a land where we can be proud and not afraid to tell the world we are Jewish. It fills my heart with such pride," he said.

When they got back to the car, he kissed her then opened her door. Before she got in, she turned and put her hands on his face and kissed him passionately.

"That was as wonderful and as magical as you said it would be," she said, as they began to drive away.

He laughed. "The waterfall was only the beginning. I have another surprise for you.

We're not going back to the kibbutz just yet."

"Really, Dovi? What is it?"

"If I told you what it is, it wouldn't be a surprise," he said and winked at her.

They drove for a while until they arrived at a small quaint village hidden deep in the mountains. There were winding roads and all the buildings were made of stone.

"Where are we?" she asked.

"This place is called Tzvat."

"Tzvat?" She tried to pronounce it. He laughed.

"Your pronunciation was close enough for me. And guess what? A miracle happened here."

"A miracle? In Biblical times?"

"No, it was much more recently than that. It happened in 1948 when the Jewish people were fighting the War of Independence. I'll tell you exactly what happened as soon as we get to where we are going."

They drove up to a white stone building with a sign in front that said "Ari Ashkenazi Synagogue."

"We're here," Dovid said.

"At a synagogue?"

"Yes. And something very amazing happened right here." He smiled. Then he got out of the car and opened her door.

"Come," he said smiling.

The inside of the temple was magnificent. It was nowhere as large as the church that she had attended with her mother back in Warsaw, but it was unique and just as lovely. There were stained glass windows that cast rich rays of color onto the polished wood floor.

They kept walking until they saw a large hand-carved wooden arc painted in brilliant shades. It was so magnificent that Eidel let out a gasp.

"I have never seen anything so gorgeous," she said. "Just look at these carvings. This must have taken years to complete."

"It is a work of art," Dovid said. "This is the Holy Arc. You see that lion that is carved right there on the top? That is the lion of Judea; he is protecting the Torah."

"It's glorious," she said.

"That big square in the center that is covered with blue velvet and adorned with Hebrew letters written in gold and white. That is the Torah."

"Can I touch it?"

"The sign says that we must not touch the Holy Arc."

She nodded. Next to the Arc was a prayer station and a little to the right of that was what he had brought her there to see. It was a wooden wall. Several holes were in the wood and inside the holes were tiny pieces of paper pushed into them.

"This is the miracle," he said, pointing to the wall and the holes.

"This wooden wall with holes in it?" she asked, raising her eyebrows as if he had brought her to see something that was not worth their time.

"Yes. And now I am going to tell you the story," he said. "Here, come. Sit down and listen."

Eidel wasn't impressed with the wall. But when she was with Dovid she felt warm and protected. And right as he was about to tell her the story, it reminded her in a very strange and tender way of how she had felt when her mother told her Bible stories when she was a child.

Dovid began. "So," he said, hesitating for drama. "The story takes place in 1948 when our people were at war. One day, this little synagogue was filled with Jewish people praying. The rabbi was saying a special prayer and so he instructed the members to bend and sway while they were praying—the way that you have seen some of the very religious Jews sway when they daven. Then, just as the entire congregation bent over to show their devotion to God, a massive piece of shrapnel came flying through the window. But because everyone was bent over, the shrapnel flew over their heads and nobody was hurt. It landed in that wall. That is what made the holes. Had the congregants been standing, many of them would have been killed. So it was a miracle that no one at all was hurt.

"That is a miracle that it happened right at that very moment," she said.

"And today, whenever visitors come here, they can write a little prayer to God and put it inside of one of these holes…and it is said that God will answer their prayer," Dovid whispered to her softly.

"I do love you, Dovi," she said.

"I know you do and I am happy that God has blessed me with such a wonderful wife. I love you too."

"Can we leave a prayer for God?"

"Of course," he said. "I planned on it. In fact, I even came prepared. I brought a pencil and paper."

After they both finished writing their prayers and tucking them into the holes they walked back to the car.

"How did you know about this place and about the waterfall?"

"I've been asking everyone at the kibbutz what they thought I could do for you that would make you see the wonder of Israel. Ari suggested this. He even arranged it for us. I want you to be happy, Eidel. I am constantly reminded that you are so young and tender, like a child. And I love you so much that it hurts me to see you unhappy. Believe me, I know how badly you miss your mother. And I can see that the adjustment of moving here to Israel and the kibbutz has been hard for you. But I will do whatever I can for you."

"You are good to me, Dovi. I know that. Please, forgive me for being so sad and depressive lately. I am just having a hard time with the loss of my mother. I want to fit in here. I really do. But I just feel so awkward and uncomfortable."

"I know you do and that's why we're not staying. I am hoping that you will be happier in America."

"I am happy with you, Dovid. But it's hard for me to be carefree with all of the changes that have been going on in my life. Please, just be patient with me. Give me time."

"You have as much time as you need. I am devoted to you. I will be at your side forever if you will have me."

They stopped for lunch at a kosher restaurant. Then they bought some candles from a candlemaker.

"This little village of Tsvat is famous for candlemaking. And ... it's also known for mysticism and Kabbalah. The people here are very religious. That is why I asked you to dress very modestly."

"What is mysticism? Is it like magic?"

"Sort of, I think. But to be honest with you, I really don't know much about it. Kabbalah is very secretive Jewish mysticism. It takes years of study, and I have never studied it."

"It is interesting, though. I would love to know more about it."

"Yes, it is interesting. Maybe someday I will

have the time to learn more about it."

By the time they arrived back at the kibbutz, it was too late to have dinner with the rest of the group. The sun had already set and as they entered the compound they could hear singing.

"Let's go into the kitchen and get something to eat," he said.

She nodded. "I had a nice day, Dovid."

"Me too." He took her hand and they walked side by side through the main building of the kibbutz.

CHAPTER FOURTY-ONE

✡

By the end of August, the days were scorching hot. Eidel's clothes stuck to her body. She was wet with sweat as she worked in the kitchen.

She was cutting green peppers when Dovid came running in. "Make room on the table; someone got hurt in the field. I have to help him," he said.

A man came walking through the door, his face white as plaster. His hair stuck to his face with sweat. Blood covered the front of his shirt and dirty pants.

"Sit here," Dovid commanded, taking charge immediately. "Someone get me a pot with clean warm water, a bunch of rags, a bottle of whiskey, a needle and thread and some matches."

"What happened?" Eidel asked. All of the blood made her stomach queasy.

"He cut off the tip of his finger. I'm going to sew it back on."

"Oh," she said, swaying. "I think I am going to go in the other room, Dovid."

He took a moment and looked up at Eidel. Then he turned to one of the women who was standing and watching. "Take my wife into the other room. Get her a wet towel and wash her face and the back of her neck while I take care of this man."

The woman did not question him. In fact, no one did. Dovid saved a man's finger that day, and from then on everyone wanted him to stay. It was important to have a doctor readily available on the kibbutz. And even though Dovid was not a doctor with a medical degree, he had enough experience to be very useful to the members of the kibbutz.

They all knew that he and Eidel were

waiting for their visas, however, they tried desperately to convince him to stay. The women tried to include Eidel in their conversations but it was no use. When the visas came through in mid-September, Eidel was ecstatic. It wasn't Israel so much that she wanted to leave, it was life on a kibbutz. And although Dovid didn't want to go, he put Eidel's happiness first and arranged for them to sail out before the month's end.

Dovid's friends at the kibbutz gave him the names and possible locations of people they could contact once they arrived in the U.S. It seemed that the majority were located in a city called Chicago, somewhere in Illinois.

"Here, take this, look up Hyme Strassberg. I met him in the DP camp before I came to Israel. He was going to Chicago. Maybe he can help you find a place to stay or a job," someone said.

"My sister's brother-in-law is in Chicago. Here is his name and address," someone else said, handing Dovid a piece of paper.

"Listen, I knew this guy who was going to Chicago…"

Dovid took it as a sign. So many of his friends had mentioned Chicago. He doubted he would be able to find any of the contacts that had been mentioned to him. It was hard to find people; they moved around a lot. When they had first applied for their visas he thought that they might settle in New York. But everyone had said that Chicago was less crowded and it would be easier to find a job there. He discussed the situation with Eidel and she agreed that they should head to Chicago.

Before they left, Dovid took Eidel to Bethlehem. He knew she would never ask him to take her there but he also knew how much she would want to see it. She wept as they walked through the city. He didn't know what to say, so he stayed silent. Instead, he just squeezed her hand, hoping that she knew he understood how difficult it was for her to change everything in her life. He didn't know how to find the words to tell her that he respected her love of Jesus and her religious background. He wished he could feel at ease in saying "You don't have to give all of this up for me," but the truth was that he was much more comfortable with her as a Jew than as a Catholic. It was selfish. He knew it, but he couldn't help himself. Dovid did his best, but he was not perfect.

CHAPTER FOURTY-TWO

✡

It was a breezy autumn day when the Levis boarded the ship to America. Dovid turned to look back at the mountains. He wondered if he would ever see his beloved homeland again. The year or so that Dovid and Eidel had spent in Israel had been one of the most precious periods of Dovid's life, although he would never tell Eidel because he didn't want her to feel guilty about the move to America. He would always miss the wild and independent land of his people.

As he stood on the deck and looked out, he wanted to make a mental photograph of all he was leaving behind.

"Land of Abraham, Land of David, and of Solomon the Wise," he thought. "Land of my people."

The ship stirred and rocked. Eidel came up to him and slid her arm through his.

"Well, we are on our way," he said smiling at her.

"Yes," she nodded. "We are. I can't believe that we are going to America, Dovi. When I was a child, America was a country that people talked about like it was as close to Heaven as a person could get."

He nodded and patted her hand. She was excited even though the night before they left she had expressed that she was worried about getting seasick again. "It's not as hot outside right now as it was when we sailed to Israel. You won't get sick this time," Dovid assured her.

He gazed into her eyes. It was easy to see that she was happy, and he was glad that she was. Then he turned his head and glanced back again one more time at the mountains.

How majestic they are, he thought, and he

remembered the battle at Masada. He also recalled how God had used Moses to part the Red Sea so that his brother, Aaron, could lead the Jewish people to the promised land. Such a rich history this land of Israel held. For him, it had been an experience that brought him back to his roots, back to his people. And he was grateful to have spent the time in this magical, wonderful land.

The ship began to sail out of the harbor. Dovid put his arm around his wife as a soft breeze danced through her lovely golden hair.

"And so, my love, we begin another chapter of our lives. I am excited for the new adventure," he said. And even though he would miss the glory of Israel, he was eager to see what lie ahead in America.

New Life, New Land

Book Three in the I Am Proud To Be A Jew series.

When Jewish Holocaust survivors Eidel and Dovid Levi arrive in the United States, they believe that their struggles are finally over. Both have suffered greatly under the Nazi reign and are ready to leave the past behind. They arrive in this new and different land filled with optimism for their future. However, acclimating into a new way of life can be challenging for immigrants. And, not only are they immigrants but they are Jewish. Although Jews are not being murdered in the United States, as they were under Hitler in Europe, the Levi's will learn that America is not without anti-Semitism. Still, they go forth, with unfathomable courage. In New Life, New Land, this young couple will face the trials and tribulations of becoming Americans and building a home for themselves and their children that will follow them.

AUTHORS NOTE

✡

First and foremost, I want to thank you for reading my novel and for your continued interest in my work. From time to time, I receive emails from my readers that contest the accuracy of my events. When you pick up a novel, you are entering the author's world where we sometimes take artistic license and ask you to suspend your disbelief. I always try to keep as true to history as possible; however, sometimes there are discrepancies within my novels. This happens sometimes to keep the drama of the story. Thank you for indulging me.

I always enjoy hearing from my readers. Your feelings about my work are very important to me. If you enjoyed it, please consider telling your friends or posting a short review on Amazon. Word of mouth is an author's best friend.

If you enjoyed this book, please sign up for my mailing list, and you will receive Free short stories including an USA Today award-winning novella as my gift to you!!!!! To sign up, just go to…

www.RobertaKagan.com

Many blessings to you,

Roberta

Email: roberta@robertakagan.com

Come and like my Facebook page!

https://www.facebook.com/roberta.kagan.9

Join my book club

https://www.facebook.com/groups/1494285400798292/?ref=br_rs

Follow me on BookBub to receive automatic emails whenever I am offering a special price, a freebie, a giveaway, or a new release. Just click the link below, then click follow button to the right of my name. Thank you so much for your interest in my work.

https://www.bookbub.com/authors/roberta-kagan.

MORE BOOKS BY THE AUTHOR AVAILABLE ON AMAZON

Not In America

Book One in A Jewish Family Saga

"Jews drink the blood of Christian babies. They use it for their rituals. They are evil and they consort with the devil."

These words rang out in 1928 in a small town in upstate New York when little four-year-old Evelyn Wilson went missing. A horrible witch hunt ensued that was based on a terrible folk tale known as the blood libel.

Follow the Schatzman's as their son is accused of the most horrific crime imaginable. This accusation destroys their family and sends their mother and sister on a journey home to Berlin just as the Nazi's are about to come to power.

Not in America is based on true events. However, the author has taken license in her work, creating a what if tale that could easily have been true.

They Never Saw It Coming

Book Two in A Jewish Family Saga

Goldie Schatzman is nearing forty, but she is behaving like

a reckless teenager, and every day she is descending deeper into a dark web. Since her return home to Berlin, she has reconnected with her childhood friend, Leni, a free spirit who has swept Goldie into the Weimar lifestyle that is overflowing with artists and writers, but also with debauchery. Goldie had spent the last nineteen years living a dull life with a spiritless husband. And now she has been set free, completely abandoning any sense of morals she once had.

As Goldie's daughter, Alma, is coming of marriageable age, her grandparents are determined to find her a suitable match. But will Goldie's life of depravity hurt Alma's chances to find a Jewish husband from a good family?

And all the while the SA, a preclude to the Nazi SS, is gaining strength. Germany is a hotbed of political unrest. Leaving a nightclub one night, Goldie finds herself caught in the middle of a demonstration that has turned violent. She is rescued by Felix, a member of the SA, who is immediately charmed by her blonde hair and Aryan appearance. Goldie is living a lie, and her secrets are bound to catch up with her. A girl, who she'd scorned in the past, is now a proud member of the Nazi Party and still carries a deep-seated vendetta against Goldie.

On the other side of the Atlantic, Sam is thriving with the Jewish mob in Manhattan; however, he has made a terrible mistake. He has destroyed the trust of the woman he believes is his bashert. He knows he cannot live without her, and he is desperately trying to find a way to win her heart.

And Izzy, the man who Sam once called his best friend, is now his worst enemy. They are both in love with the same woman, and the competition between them could easily result in death.

Then Sam receives word that something has happened in Germany, and he must accompany his father on a journey across the ocean. He is afraid that if he leaves before his beloved accepts his proposal, he might lose her forever.

When The Dust Settled

Book Three in A Jewish Family Saga

Coming December 2020

As the world races like a runaway train toward World War 11, the Schatzman family remains divided.

In New York, prohibition has ended, and Sam's world is turned upside down. He has been earning a good living transporting illegal liquor for the Jewish mob. Now that alcohol is legal, America is celebrating. But as the liquor flows freely, the mob boss realizes he must expand his illegal interests if he is going to continue to live the lavish lifestyle he's come to know. Some of the jobs Sam is offered go against his moral character. Transporting alcohol was one thing, but threatening lives is another.

Meanwhile, across the ocean in Italy, Mussolini, a heartless dictator, runs the country with an iron fist. Those who speak out against him disappear and are never seen again. For the first time since that horrible incident in Medina, Alma is finally happy and has fallen in love with a kind and generous Italian doctor who already has a job awaiting him in Rome;

however, he is not Jewish. Alma must decide whether to marry him and risk disappointing her bubbie or let him go to find a suitable Jewish match.

In Berlin, the Nazis are quickly rising to power. Flags with swastikas are appearing everywhere. And Dr. Goebbels, the minister of propaganda is openly spewing hideous lies designed to turn the German people against the Jews. Adolf Hitler had disposed of his enemies, and the SA has been replaced by the even more terrifying SS. After the horrors they witnessed during Kristallnacht, Goldie's mother, Esther, is ready to abandon all she knows to escape the country. She begs her husband to leave Germany. But Ted refuses to leave everything that he spent his entire life working for. At what point is it too late to leave? And besides, where would they go? What would they do?

The Nazis have taken the country by the throat, and the electrifying atmosphere of the Weimar a distant memory. The period of artistic tolerance and debauchery has been replaced by a strict and cruel regime that seeks to destroy all who do not fit its ideal. Goldie's path of depravity is catching up with her, and her secrets are threatened. Will her Nazi enemies finally strike?

Book Four in A Jewish Family Saga

Coming Early 2021....

The Smallest Crack

Book One in a Holocaust Story series.

1933 Berlin, Germany

The son of a rebbe, Eli Kaetzel, and his beautiful but timid wife, Rebecca, find themselves in danger as Hitler rises to power. Eli knows that their only chance for survival may lie in the hands of Gretchen, a spirited Aryan girl. However, the forbidden and dangerous friendship between Eli and Gretchen has been a secret until now. Because, for Eli, if it is discovered that he has been keeping company with a woman other than his wife it will bring shame to him and his family. For Gretchen her friendship with a Jew is forbidden by law and could cost her, her life.

The Darkest Canyon

Book Two in a Holocaust Story series.

Nazi Germany.

Gretchen Schmidt has a secret life. She is in love with a married Jewish man. She is hiding him while his wife is posing as an Aryan woman.

Her best friend, Hilde, who unbeknownst to Gretchen is a sociopath, is working as a guard at Ravensbruck concentration camp.

If Hilde discovers Gretchen's secret, will their friendship be strong enough to keep Gretchen safe? Or will Hilde fall under the spell of the Nazis and turn her best friend over to the Gestapo?

The *Darkest Canyon* is a terrifying ride along the edge of a canyon in the dark of night.

Millions Of Pebbles

Book Three in a Holocaust Story series.

Benjamin Rabinowitz's life is shattered as he watches his wife, Lila, and his son, Moishe, leave to escape the Lodz ghetto. He is conflicted because he knows this is their best chance of survival, but he asks himself, will he ever see them again?

Ilsa Guhr has a troubled childhood, but as she comes of age, she learns that her beauty and sexuality give her the power to get what she wants. But she craves an even greater power. As the Nazis take control of Germany, she sees an opportunity to gain everything she's ever desired.

Fate will weave a web that will bring these two unlikely people into each other's lives.

Sarah and Solomon

Book Four in a Holocaust Story series

"Give me your children" -Chaim Mordechaj Rumkowski. September 1942 The Lodz Ghetto.

When Hitler's Third Reich reined with an iron fist, the head Judenrat of the Lodz ghetto decides to comply with the Nazis. He agrees to send the Jewish children off on a transport to face death.

In order to save her two young children a mother must take the ultimate risk. The night before the children are to rounded up and sent to their deaths, she helps her nine year old son and her five year old daughter escape into a war torn Europe. However, she cannot fit through the barbed wire, and so the children must go alone.

Follow Sarah and Solomon as they navigate their way through a world filled with hatred, and treachery. However, even in the darkest hour there is always a flicker of light. And these two young innocent souls will be aided by people who's lights will always shine in our memories.

All My Love, Detrick

Book One in the All My Love, Detrick series.

Book One in the All My Love, Detrick Series

Can Forbidden Love Survive in Nazi Germany?

After Germany's defeat in the First World War, she lays in ruins, falling beneath the wheel of depression and famine. And so, with a promise of restoring Germany to her rightful place as a world power, Adolf Hitler begins to rise.

Detrick, a handsome seventeen-year-old Aryan boy is reluctant to join the Nazi party because of his friendship with Jacob, who is Jewish and has been like a father figure to him. However, he learns that in order to protect the woman he loves, Jacob's daughter, he must abandon all his principles and join the Nazis. He knows the only way to survive is to live a double life. Detrick is confronted with fear every day; if he is discovered, he and those he loves will come face to face with the ultimate cruelty of the Third Reich.

Follow two families, one Jewish and one German, as they are thrust into a world of danger on the eve of the Nazis rise to power.

You Are My Sunshine

Book Two in the All My Love, Detrick series.

A child's innocence is the purest of all.

In Nazi Germany, Helga Haswell is at a crossroads. She's pregnant by a married SS officer who has since abandoned her. Left alone with the thought of raising a fatherless child, she has nowhere to turn -- until the Lebensborn steps in. They will take Helga's child when it's born and raise it as their own. Helga will now be free to live her life.

But when Helga has second thoughts, it's already too late. The papers are signed, and her claim to her child has been revoked. Her daughter belongs to Hitler now. And when Hitler's delusions of grandeur rapidly accelerate, Germany becomes involved in a two-front war against the heroic West and the fearless Russians.

Helga's child seems doomed to a life raised by the cruelest humans on Earth. But God's plan for her sends the young girl to the most unexpected people. In their warm embrace, she's given the chance for love in a world full of hate.

You Are My Sunshine is the heartfelt story of second chances. Helga Haswell may be tied to an unthinkable past, but her young daughter has the chance of a brighter future.

The Promised Land:

From Nazi Germany to Israel

Book Three in the All My Love, Detrick series.

Zofia Weiss, a Jewish woman with a painful past, stands at the dock, holding the hand of a little girl. She is about to board The SS Exodus, bound for Palestine with only her life, a dream, and a terrifying secret. As her eyes scan the crowds of people, she sees a familiar face. Her heart pounds and beads of sweat form on her forehead…

The Nazis have surrendered. Zofia survived the Holocaust, but she lives in constant fear. The one person who knows her dark secret is a sadistic SS officer with the power to destroy the life she's working so hard to rebuild. Will he ever find her and the innocent child she has sworn to protect?

To Be An Israeli

Book Four in the All My Love, Detrick series.

Elan understands what it means to be an Israeli. He's sacrificed the woman he loved, his marriage, and his life for Israel. When Israel went to war and Elan was summoned in the middle of the night, he did not hesitate to defend his country, even though he knew he might pay a terrible price. Elan is not a perfect man by any means. He can be cruel. He can be stubborn and self-righteous. But he is brave, and he loves more deeply than he will ever admit.

This is his story.

However, it is not only his story; it is also the story of the lives of the women who loved him: Katja, the girl whom he cherished but could never marry, who would haunt him forever. Janice, the spoiled American he wed to fill a void, who would keep a secret from him that would one day shatter his world. And…Nina, the beautiful Mossad agent whom Elan longed to protect but knew he never could.

To Be an Israeli spans from the beginning of the Six-Day War in 1967 through 1986 when a group of American tourists are on their way to visit their Jewish homeland.

Forever My Homeland

The Fifth and final book in the All My Love, Detrick series.

Bari Lynn has a secret. So she, a young Jewish-American girl, decides to tour Israel with her best friend and the members of their synagogue in search of answers.

Meanwhile, beneath the surface in Israel, trouble is stirring with a group of radical Islamists.

The case falls into the hands of Elan, a powerful passionate Mossad agent, trying to pick up the pieces of his shattered life. He believes nothing can break him, but in order to achieve their goals, the terrorists will go to any means to bring Elan to his knees.

Forever, My Homeland is the story of a country built on blood and determination. It is the tale of a strong and courageous people who don't have the luxury of backing down from any fight, because they live with the constant memory of the Holocaust. In the back of their minds, there is always a soft voice that whispers "Never again."

Michal's Destiny

Book One in the Michal's Destiny series.

It is 1919 in Siberia. Michal—a young, sheltered girl—has eyes for a man other than her betrothed. For a young girl growing up in a traditional Jewish settlement, an arranged marriage is a fact of life. However, destiny, it seems, has other plans for Michal. When a Cossack pogrom invades her small village, the protected life Michal has grown accustomed to and loves will crumble before her eyes. Everything she knows is gone and she is forced to leave her home and embark on a journey to Berlin with the man she thought she wanted. Michal faces love, loss, and heartache because she is harboring a secret that threatens to destroy her every attempt at happiness. But over the next fourteen tumultuous years, during the peak of the Weimar Republic, she learns she is willing to do anything to have the love she longs for and to protect her family.

However, it is now 1933. Life in Berlin is changing, especially for the Jews. Dark storm clouds are looming on the horizon. Adolf Hitler is about to become the chancellor of Germany, and that will change everything for Michal forever.

A Family Shattered

Book Two in the Michal's Destiny series.

In book two of the Michal's Destiny series, Tavvi and Michal have problems in the beginning of their relationship, but they build a life together. Each stone is laid carefully with love and mutual understanding. They now have a family with two beautiful daughters and a home full of happiness.

It is now 1938—Kristallnacht. Blood runs like a river on the streets, shattered glass covers the walkways of Jewish shop owners, and gangs of Nazi thugs charge though Berlin in a murderous rage. When Tavvi, the strong-willed Jewish carpenter, races outside, without thinking of his own welfare, to save his daughters fiancée, little does his wife Michal know that she might never hold him in her arms again. In an instant, all the stones they laid together come crashing down leaving them with nothing but the hope of finding each other again.

Watch Over My Child

Book Three in the Michal's Destiny series.

In book three of the Michal's Destiny series, after her parents are arrested by the Nazis on Kristallnacht, twelve-year-old Gilde Margolis is sent away from her home, her sister, and everyone she knows and loves.

Alone and afraid, Gilde boards a train through the Kindertransport bound for London, where she will stay with strangers. Over the next seven years as Gilde is coming of age, she learns about love, friendship, heartache, and the pain of betrayal. As the Nazis grow in power, London is thrust into a brutal war against Hitler. Severe rationing is imposed upon the British, while air raids instill terror, and bombs all but destroy the city. Against all odds, and with no knowledge of what has happened to her family in Germany, Gilde keeps a tiny flicker of hope buried deep in her heart: someday, she will be reunited with her loved ones.

Another Breath, Another Sunrise

Book Four, the final book in the Michal's Destiny series.

Now that the Reich has fallen, in this—the final book of the Michal's Destiny series—the reader follows the survivors as they find themselves searching to reconnect with those they love. However, they are no longer the people they were before the war.

While the Russian soldiers, who are angry with the German people and ready to pillage, beat, and rape, begin to invade what's left of Berlin, Lotti is alone and fears for her life.

Though Alina Margolis has broken every tradition to become a successful business woman in America, she fears what has happened to her family and loved ones across the Atlantic Ocean.

As the curtain pulls back on Gilde, a now successful actress in London, she realizes that all that glitters is not gold, and she longs to find the lost family the Nazi's had stolen from her many years ago.

This is a story of ordinary people whose lives were shattered by the terrifying ambitions of Adolf Hitler—a true madman.

And ... Who Is The Real Mother?

Book One in the Eidel's Story series.

In the Bible, there is a story about King Solomon, who was said to be the wisest man of all time. The story goes like this:

Two women came to the king for advice. Both of them were claiming to be the mother of a child. The king took the child in his arms and said, "I see that both of you care for this child very much. So, rather than decide which of you is the real mother, I will cut the child in half and give each of you a half."

One of the women agreed to the king's decision, but the other cried out, "NO, give the child to that other woman. Don't hurt my baby."

"Ahh," said the king to the second woman who refused to cut the baby. "I will give the child to you, because the real mother would sacrifice anything for her child. She would even give her baby away to another woman if it meant sparing the baby from pain."

And so, King Solomon gave the child to his rightful mother.

The year is 1941. The place is the Warsaw Ghetto in Poland.

The ghetto is riddled with disease and starvation. Children are dying every day.

Zofia Weiss, a young mother, must find a way to save, Eidel her only child. She negotiates a deal with a man on the black market to smuggle Eidel out in the middle of the night and deliver her to Helen, a Polish woman who is a good friend of Zofia's. It is the ultimate sacrifice because there is a good chance that Zofia will die without ever seeing her precious child again.

Helen has a life of her own, a husband and a son. She takes Eidel to live with her family even though she and those she loves will face terrible danger every day. Helen will be forced to do unimaginable things to protect all that she holds dear. And as Eidel grows up in Helen's warm maternal embrace, Helen finds that she has come to love the little girl with all her heart.

So, when Zofia returns to claim her child, and King Solomon is not available to be consulted, it is the reader who must decide…

Who is the real mother?

Secrets Revealed

Book Two in the Eidel's Story series.

Hitler has surrendered. The Nazi flags, which once hung throughout the city striking terror in the hearts of Polish citizens, have been torn down. It seems that Warsaw should be rejoicing in its newly found freedom, but Warsaw is not free. Instead, it is occupied by the Soviet Union, held tight in Stalin's iron grip. Communist soldiers, in uniform, now control the city. Where once people feared the dreaded swastika, now they tremble at the sight of the hammer and sickle. It is a treacherous time. And in the midst of all this danger, Ela Dobinski, a girl with a secret that could change her life, is coming of age.

New Life, New Land

Book Three in the Eidel's Story series.

When Jewish Holocaust survivors Eidel and Dovid Levi arrive in the United States, they believe that their struggles are finally over. Both have suffered greatly under the Nazi reign and are ready to leave the past behind. They arrive in this new and different land filled with optimism for their future. However, acclimating into a new way of life can be challenging for immigrants. And, not only are they immigrants but they are Jewish. Although Jews are not being murdered in the United States, as they were under Hitler in Europe, the Levi's will learn that America is not without anti-Semitism. Still, they go forth, with unfathomable courage. In New Life, New Land, this young couple will face the trials and tribulations of becoming Americans and building a home for themselves and their children that will follow them.

Another Generation

Book Four in the Eidel's Story series.

In the final book in the Eidel's Story series the children of Holocaust survivors Eidel and Dovid Levi have grown to adulthood. They each face hard trials and tribulations of their own, many of which stem from growing up as children of Holocaust survivors. Haley is a peacemaker who yearns to please even at the expense of her own happiness. Abby is an angry rebel on the road to self-destruction. And, Mark, Dovid's only son, carries a heavy burden of guilt and secrets.

He wants to please his father, but he cannot. Each of the Levi children must find a way to navigate their world while accepting that the lessons they have learned from the parents, both good and bad, have shaped them into the people they are destined to become.

The Wrath Of Eden

The Wrath of Eden Book One.

Deep in them Appalachian hills, far from the main roads where the citified people come and go, lies a harsh world where a man's character is all he can rightly claim as his own. This here is a land of deep, dark coal mines, where a miner ain't certain when he ventures into the belly of the mountain whether he will ever see daylight again. To this very day, they still tell tales of the Robin Hood-like outlaw Pretty Boy Floyd, even though there ain't no such thing as a thousand dollar bill no more From this beautiful yet dangerous country where folks is folks comes a story as old as time itself; a tale of good and evil, of right and wrong, and of a troubled man who walked a perilous path on his journey back to God.

The Wrath of Eden begins in 1917, in the fictitious town of Mudwater Creek, West Virginia. Mudwater lies deep in mining country in the Appalachian Mountains. Here, the eldest son of a snake-handling preacher, Cyrus Hunt, is emotionally broken by what he believes is his father's favoritism toward his brother, Aiden. Cyrus is so hurt by what he believes is his father's lack of love for him that he runs away from home to seek his fortune. Not only will he fight in the Great War, but he will return to America and then ramble around the United States for several years, right through the great depression. While on his journey, Cyrus will encounter a multitude of colorful characters and from each he will learn more about himself. This is a tale of good and evil, of brother against brother, of the intricate web of family, and of love lost and found again.

The Angels Song

The Wrath of Eden Book Two.

Cyrus Hunt returns home to the Appalachian Mountains after years of traveling. He has learned a great deal about himself from his journey, and he realizes that the time has come to make peace with his brother and his past. When he arrives in the small town where he grew up, he finds that he has a granddaughter that he never knew existed, and she is almost the same age as his daughter. The two girls grow up as close as sisters. But one is more beautiful than a star-filled night sky, while the other has a physical condition that keeps her from spreading her wings and discovering her own self-worth. As the girls grow into women, the love they have for each other is constantly tested by sibling rivalry, codependency, and betrayals. Are these two descendents of Cyrus Hunt destined to repeat their father's mistakes? Or will they rise above their human weakness and inadequacies and honor the bonds of blood and family that unite them?

One Last Hope

A Voyage to Escape Nazi Germany

Formerly *The Voyage*

Inspired by True Events

On May 13, 1939, five strangers boarded the MS St. Louis. Promised a future of safety away from Nazi Germany and Hitler's Third Reich, unbeknownst to them they were about to embark upon a voyage built on secrets, lies, and treachery. Sacrifice, love, life, and death hung in the balance as each fought against fate, but the voyage was just the beginning.

A Flicker Of Light

Hitler's Master Plan.

The year is 1943

The forests of Munich are crawling with danger during the rule of the Third Reich, but in order to save the life of her unborn child, Petra Jorgenson must escape from the Lebensborn Institute. She is alone, seven months pregnant, and penniless. Avoiding the watchful eyes of the armed guards in the overhead tower, she waits until the dead of night and then climbs under the flesh-shredding barbed wire surrounding the Institute. At the risk of being captured and murdered, she runs headlong into the terrifying, desolate woods. Even during one of the darkest periods in the history of mankind, when horrific acts of cruelty become commonplace and Germany seemed to have gone crazy under the direction of a madman, unexpected heroes come to light. And although there are those who would try to destroy true love, it will prevail. Here in this lost land ruled by human monsters, Petra will learn that even when one faces what appears to be the end of the world, if one looks hard enough, one will find that there is always A Flicker of Light.

The Heart Of A Gypsy

If you liked Inglorious Basterds, Pulp Fiction, and Django Unchained, you'll love The Heart of a Gypsy!

During the Nazi occupation, bands of freedom fighters roamed the forests of Eastern Europe. They hid while waging their own private war against Hitler's tyrannical and murderous reign. Among these Resistance fighters were several groups of Romany people (Gypsies).

The Heart of a Gypsy is a spellbinding love story. It is a tale of a man with remarkable courage and the woman who loved him more than life itself. This historical novel is filled with romance and spiced with the beauty of the Gypsy culture.

Within these pages lies a tale of a people who would rather die than surrender their freedom. Come, enter into a little-known world where only a few have traveled before . . . the world of the Romany.

If you enjoy romance, secret magical traditions, and riveting action you will love The Heart of a Gypsy.

Please be forewarned that this book contains explicit scenes of a sexual nature.

Printed in Great Britain
by Amazon